Gwen's Honor

To: Speedy Guthrie

Best Wishes,
Sandra Wilkins

GWEN'S HONOR

Sandra Wilkins

Montlake
Romance

Text copyright © 2013 Sandra Wilkins

Published by Montlake Romance
P.O. Box 400818
Las Vegas, NV 89140

ISBN-13: 9781612186917
ISBN-10: 1612186912

To my parents—Dale and Janice Broudrick.
For Dad and our mutual admiration of the Emerald Isle
and to Mom for passing along her love of books.

PROLOGUE

September 18, 1906
Oklahoma Territory

Josh Flynn tipped his gray wool cap over his eyes and lounged back in his seat on the No. 12 Rock Island passenger train. The northbound engine had recently passed through a town called Kingfisher. The rocking motion of the train always made him sleepy, and at eight thirty in the morning, he wanted to doze.

He'd had a nice trip to Fort Worth to visit his sister, Beth, her husband, and their new baby boy. It didn't seem like his little sister was old enough to be starting a family, but if he had just turned twenty-six, that would make her twenty. Where had the years gone?

Except for a good job with the Rock Island up in Horton, Kansas, what did he have to show for himself? No wife, no children. No Gwen. He had been separated from his childhood sweetheart, Gwen Sanders, long ago. He guessed he had only been kidding himself that he would find her someday.

Suddenly the train lurched. The engineer had thrown on the air brakes. A sickening sound of grinding metal and heavy timbers falling assaulted his ears. Josh sat up and looked out his open window in time to see the engine plunge from a flood-damaged bridge into the swirling reddish-brown water of the river.

There was no time to react as the tender, baggage, mail, smoker, and day coaches followed the engine into the current. Women and children screamed and men shouted as the day coach Josh was riding in crashed onto its side, floated in the rushing water, and then turned and lodged against the riverbank. For the moment, the car was not totally submerged. The row of windows on his side of the car was now the ceiling.

"Open the windows!" Josh shouted.

Men hurried to open any closed windows. Dark water spewed in all of the other openings. Crawling out of his window, he stood on the side of the rocking coach. He reached down and grabbed a scared child from his terrified mother. He tossed the boy onto the muddy bank, reached back in, and helped the mother out. She clambered across the car, jumped, and collapsed next to her son.

Time after time, he and a few other men assisted passengers out of the coach. After it appeared everyone was safe, he tried to make his way across the slippery car. A monstrous groan emanated from the bowels of the coach, and it shuddered. He lost his footing. He tried to stop himself from falling and cracked his arm against the side as he plummeted into the churning river.

He was so close to the bank, but he wasn't sure he could make it. Pain shot through his right arm as he tried to swim toward the shore, but he didn't seem to be making any headway. His clothes were weighing him down. His head went under into the dark abyss. An image of young Gwen's smiling face flashed in his mind. He kicked his legs furiously, and his face was above water again. He sputtered and coughed and somehow was able to see a piece of lumber being held out to him.

He grasped the wood, knowing his life depended on it. The two men on shore struggled to pull him in. When he reached the weeds, he clawed his way through the mud that was like quicksand. Four hands finally grabbed him and hauled him to safety.

He lay flat on his back, exhausted, and stared up at the gray sky. "Thank you, God," he breathed.

The bystanders tried to fuss over him, but all he could think of was Gwen. He had been given a second chance to live. He would find her as he had promised her years ago. He would search for her until his dying day.

He closed his eyes. He could feel blackness engulfing him. "I'll find you, Gwen," he whispered. "I'll find you."

CHAPTER ONE

"It's time to decide on a date, Gwen," Walter Manning stated as he sat behind his desk at the law office where he was a junior partner. He opened his appointment book.

"I agree," Gwen Sanders said enthusiastically. Her long brown-and-green plaid merino wool skirt swished as she followed him and peered over his shoulder. She still wanted to write that novel before she got married. She wondered how much longer Walter would be willing to wait. Not long by the looks of things. She wasn't sure how quickly she could write an entire book, but she took a stab at a month anyway. "How about a July wedding?"

"No. It will be infernally hot." He flipped through the pages.

"What about September?" she asked as she toyed with the stiff linen collar on her white shirtwaist.

"That promises to be a busy month for me."

"Did you have a date in mind?"

"I was thinking the end of November, if that's agreeable with you?" He glanced up at her.

"Yes. That's fine with me."

Walter dipped a pen into an ink bottle and wrote her name in the square on the last Saturday of the month. As the ink seeped into the page, she felt an odd sensation at seeing the date set in such a permanent way. It surely couldn't be wedding nerves already. She decided to ignore the heat in her cheeks.

He removed his eyeglasses, placed them in the tan leather case, and returned them to the inside pocket of his navy-blue wool suit coat. He smoothed the sides of his neatly trimmed blond hair, assuring that every strand was in place.

He rolled his chair back and stood. Tall and broad shouldered, his physique was reminiscent of a blacksmith, which was his father's profession, but he had the face of a scholar who took life seriously. There was a hint of satisfaction in his gray eyes.

"I'm pleased that's taken care of," he commented.

"Yes. I am too." She couldn't help but calculate that she had about seven months to write her book. Grinning, she took his large hands in her own and squeezed them. "So where are we going for our honeymoon? I've always dreamed of having a grand European tour."

"Surely you're not serious?"

"Why not?" She wasn't entirely serious, but she thought she would take the opportunity to voice her opinion while she had the chance. "I've always wanted to go. I would love to see the places I've read about in Great Britain, Italy, and France. I know it would be expensive, but I'm willing to forsake some luxuries when we're first married to be able to afford it."

"It's not a matter of expense, Gwendolyn. I am more than capable of providing us with an extravagant lifestyle." He pulled away from her and crossed his arms. "But I'm American and proud of it. I don't see any reason to visit Europe or spend my money there."

"Oh…" She tried not to let her disappointment show. Realistically, she hadn't been expecting him to agree, but to receive such an emphatic rejection of her secret desire left her feeling bereft.

He seemed concerned for her as he placed his hands on her shoulders. "How about we spend a week or so in Hot Springs?"

"Arkansas?" It wasn't quite as exotic as she had hoped for, but Arkansas was a pretty state. "Yes, Walter, that would be lovely."

He kissed her quickly on the mouth and held her lightly. "Good. You know I only want your happiness, don't you? That's why I agreed some time ago to let you move temporarily to Shawnee and work for that newspaper."

"I know, and I truly appreciate it. I really enjoy being the society reporter for the *Shawnee Globe*."

"You do realize you have been gone for two and a half years, don't you?"

"Has it been that long?" She was truly amazed at how quickly the time had passed.

He put his forefinger under her chin. "Your sporadic visits aren't enough any longer. People are beginning to talk."

"Who's talking?" She jerked her chin away and held it high.

"It doesn't matter who. What matters is *what* they are saying."

"And what would that be?" Her dander was up now.

"Your honor is being questioned."

"My honor? How?" She put her hands on her hips.

He looked her in the eye and said bluntly, "It is being suggested that you don't intend to marry me because you have another reason for staying in Shawnee."

"And what's that?" She glared.

"A man," he answered.

"Oh, for goodness' sakes. You know that's not true."

He didn't speak.

"You know that isn't true, don't you?"

His eyebrows rose in a silent question.

She felt deflated. "Walter, I don't like anyone, especially you, doubting my integrity. There hasn't been anyone else and there won't be anyone else for me but you." Tears threatened to fall. She hated crying.

"I trust you, Gwen." He pulled her close and put his arms around her again. "But that doesn't mean I'm not ready for your return. When *will* you move back to Guthrie?"

"Can I have a few more months?" She thought of her cousin, Luke Logan. "Luke and Ada's baby will be born soon, and it would also give me time to settle things there," she said with her cheek against the rough material of his jacket.

"All right," he agreed. "I can wait a little longer."

There was a quick rap at the door. Walter hastily placed Gwen at a respectable distance to his side before he said, "Come in."

Walter's new secretary, Tina Randolph, poked her head in and said in her cheery manner, "Just a reminder that it's almost time for Gwen's train."

"Thank you, Miss Randolph."

"You're welcome, Mr. Manning." She gave them an impish grin and closed the door.

Gwen had graduated from high school with Tina. She was better known as Teeny by the boys in their class because of her petite stature. Gwen would never admit it out loud, but she had always been a tad envious of Tina's blonde hair, blue eyes, and dainty figure. For the longest time, Gwen hadn't appreciated her own brown hair and brown eyes because of all the adoration for Teeny in school. But all that was in the past, and she would have to get over the fact that the greatest coquette she knew was working for her fiancé.

"I have an immense amount of work to do, Gwen. You don't mind going to the station by yourself, do you?"

"Oh, well, no. I suppose not. Mama sent my trunk down this morning." She was disappointed that he couldn't take the time to see her off, but tried not to show it. She guessed she would have to get used to his dedication to his profession.

"Good." He gave her a peck on the cheek and walked her toward the door. "I'll telephone you in a few days."

She picked up her black leather traveling bag from a chair. "I'll be back before you know it."

"I'll hold you to that." He smiled as he opened the door for her.

She went out into the small waiting area with taupe walls and expensive decor. She passed by Tina's desk as she walked out into the hallway that joined all of the offices.

"Have a good trip!" Tina said with bubbly generosity as she got up from her chair.

"I will," she assured her.

Gwen glanced back and tried to forget the image of Walter and Tina standing side by side.

~

Gwen was about halfway home, at the station in Oklahoma City waiting in a passenger car seat for the remaining passengers to board. It was such a relief to leave Guthrie. She always felt she had to be so formal and refined around her mother and Walter. She didn't want to mull over the fact that she would soon have to be that way for the rest of her living days. So she turned her attention instead to the other travelers. Observing people was a pastime of hers, but she tried to be discreet by peeping out from under the brim of her wide-brimmed straw hat.

A young couple who could barely keep their eyes off each other, apparently newlyweds, found a cozy spot and remained oblivious to anyone else on the train. A cranky elderly woman followed with her cane thumping on the floor as she moved down the aisle. The next one to board was a self-assured, handsome young man.

He was thin and fit and dressed simply in tan work pants, a light-blue shirt, and a brown corduroy jacket. His jet-black hair was neatly trimmed, although it was a tad longer than the norm, as were his sideburns. As he neared, she could see that his eyes were the darkest of browns, like the color of strong coffee. There was something familiar about him, but she couldn't quite put her finger on it. She traveled so much, she probably had seen him somewhere before. But then, no, she reasoned. She would remember someone as striking as him.

It amused her that he tipped his brown flat-topped railroad hat to every female on board. She averted her gaze when he caught her eye and grinned at her.

He dropped into the seat across the aisle from her. "Good afternoon, miss."

She nodded politely, but didn't respond.

"It's a fine day to be sure," he commented.

Gwen's interest was piqued when he spoke. His voice was deep and melodic, but what intrigued her was his accent. She prided herself on being able to discern a person's origins by his or her inflections.

"Yes, it is," she agreed. She secretly wanted him to talk more, but she also didn't want to be too friendly to a strange man.

"Me own sainted grandmother used to say this was the kind of weather that would make the wee lambs frolic with joy across the glens," he mused.

"Hmm." She tried not to seem interested, even though she was.

Irish! That was it! He had the slightest hint of an Irish brogue in his Midwestern American accent. She would know it anywhere. When her family first moved to Guthrie, they had rented a little house next door to an Irish family.

She had been great friends with their son, Josh Flynn, from about the age of eleven to fifteen. Once upon a time, she'd even had romantic notions about him. But then her father had been hired by a surveying crew with the Santa Fe Railroad and she had to leave. She and Josh had promised to write, and he vowed to find her again someday when they were older. Her family followed her father, living in hotel after hotel until their mother had had enough and they moved back to Guthrie about a year later. Upon their return, Gwen found that Josh's family had packed up and left. Someone from the old neighborhood said the Flynns had gone back to Kansas City, and Gwen never heard another word from Josh.

She was brought out of her reverie by the stranger's voice.

"I'm afraid I'm being a bother, miss. I'll plague you no longer."

"You're not really…" She waved her hand. "I'm just not accustomed to being approached by men on trains. My fiancé wouldn't appreciate it either." Thinking about Josh and all those broken promises made her irritable, but she tried not to take it out on the stranger.

Curious, she studied his features again. He had a long, thin nose and the slightest indention in his firm chin. The inquisitive side of her wondered if this man could possibly be Josh Flynn. She doubted it, but something nibbled at the back of her mind.

His generously carved lips held a ready smile. "Beg pardon, miss." He seemed appropriately penitent. "Your man would have every right to want to protect such a lovely young lady as yourself."

She was trying to decide whether to laugh at his compliment when two loud, long blasts from the locomotive pierced the air. The passenger car pitched as it began to roll forward.

The man next to her unabashedly made the sign of the cross and murmured a prayer under his breath. Gwen was taken aback by his public display of faith. A lot of men she knew would leave that at the church door.

"Don't you feel train travel is safe?" she couldn't help asking.

"I did until September last." He gave her a flimsy smile.

"September? Wasn't that when that train fell into the Cimarron River after the bridge failed?"

"Yes."

"You weren't on it, were you?" Gwen was aghast.

"Aye. I was. 'Twas a tragic thing to live through, and when I think of the souls that were lost…" He shuddered. His speech pattern lapsed into that of his forebears as his face became weary.

It was a face that Gwen instantly realized she did recognize. Her heart gave a strange little flip-flop in her chest. "I read a list of the injured in the newspaper and saw the name of an old friend, Josh Flynn. I've wondered ever since if it truly was him and if he recovered." She awaited his reaction.

He gaped at her for a moment and then studied her with furrowed black eyebrows. "Gwen? Gwen Sanders?" He seemed amazed.

She was incredulous. "Josh? It can't be." She could definitely now see that the attractive face before her was a more masculine version of her young friend.

"Of all the times and places to meet again after all these years," she began.

"I can't believe it myself." He reached out as if to touch her, but refrained.

"How is it that you're on this particular train?" she asked. She was still finding it hard to believe it was him.

"I'm moving. I decided I wanted to see a bit of the world." He gave her a sly smile. "I was working in the Rock Island shops in Horton, Kansas. So I put in for a transfer to the yards in Shawnee. You've heard of the town?"

She couldn't help but laugh. "Yes. I've heard of it. I live there. I work for the local newspaper."

"You can't be serious?" His face held a mixture of awe and joy.

"I am. What do you do for the railroad?"

"I work in the cabinet shops. We make tables, cabinets, desks, and such."

"I didn't realize they did things like that there," she said.

"Aye. They repair the engines and the coaches, and there are also shops for painting and upholstery. They even have their own sawmill. The yards are a busy place."

"I never thought of all they must do."

"It takes a lot to make a railroad run smoothly."

She nodded. She knew he must do a fair amount of physical work. "If I remember correctly, the newspaper account of the train wreck said you had broken an arm." He appeared sound and healthy.

"That I did. I was off work for six weeks or so. It healed fine, but it aches at times." His long, lean fingers absently rubbed his right forearm. "Then there were some seasonal layoffs in Horton this winter. So I decided to investigate some other yards. Shawnee had a vacancy."

"What made you think of coming back to Oklahoma Territory?" She was curious.

"I was looking…" He paused. He stared into her eyes for a second before he grinned. "I was looking for adventures, and this wild territory seemed like the place for me."

She smiled. "It may not be untamed for long. We're trying to become a state, you know. The delegates from Oklahoma and Indian Territories have finished writing the constitution. It just has to be approved now. We may have statehood this year," she said proudly.

"You don't say?" He snapped his fingers. "It doesn't look like I'll get to sow my wild oats after all."

She chuckled. Even as a youth, Josh had been humorous, confident, and friendly. She was glad to see so many of the things she admired about him were still intact. She was so glad.

CHAPTER TWO

The engine slowed down for its arrival in Shawnee. Josh still couldn't believe he had found Gwen so easily. He had planned on starting his new job and then traveling to Guthrie to see if he could find her. He knew when he set out on this venture it might be an impossible task.

In the meantime, he had been eyeing every brunette of a certain age between Kansas and Oklahoma City. He had sat next to Gwen and chatted with her in high hopes, although he certainly hadn't known it was her right away. She seemed so sophisticated now and not much like the blossoming tomboy of a girl he'd known. She had been a comely girl with braids down her back, but now she was a beauty, with her shiny brown upswept hair. She had strong features, although they didn't overpower her face. Her brown eyes were inquisitive yet gentle as a doe's. He couldn't let himself linger over how full and kissable her lips were, because she was engaged. That had been startling news to be sure. It was quite a blow to have the rug pulled so completely out from under his feet.

He knew it wasn't wise, but he just couldn't let her disappear again. He didn't want to never see her again once the train stopped.

"I don't suppose you know of a good rooming house, do you? I need to find a nice one, preferably one that has a space for me to do some carpentry work on the side," he asked, as the engineer began to apply the brakes.

"Well, there are several around town that cater to railroad workers, but whether they would have an extra area like you need…I don't know…" She looked as if she was seriously pondering the question. "My landlady, Mrs. Brown, doesn't usually rent out to men, but there was a Mr. Vance who used to live out back above the carriage house. The carriage house is only used for storage now. We're a couple of blocks from the yards on Market Street. Maybe I could talk her into renting it again."

"That sounds perfect." He was more than thrilled at the prospect.

The conductor made his way down the aisle. "Shawnee. Next stop, Shawnee," he announced.

The train soon came to a halt. Some of the passengers began to gather their belongings and depart.

Josh stood and motioned for Gwen to lead the way. His pulse quickened as she brushed past him with a swish of skirts. She had the faint scent of soap about her. He liked that. He had never taken to women who doused themselves with perfume. As he followed her, he was able to admire her freely. Tall and shapely, Gwen carried herself with a dignified, almost scholarly air. She had always been smart. In the past, he had to be on his toes around her to keep up with all the books she read.

He had to put an end to marveling over her charms as he landed on the ground next to her. They hailed a carriage for hire and waited for their trunks to be unloaded from the train and placed on the carriage. When they were ready, Gwen gave the address to the driver.

It wasn't long before they pulled up in front of a large, white, three-story house with an average-sized front porch and sky-blue railings. He liked the look of it, not too fancy or too drab.

He paid the man, and Gwen helped him haul their trunks to the porch.

"Let's leave these here for now," Gwen huffed. "We should find Mrs. Brown first."

She opened the door, and he followed her into a small entry hall. Stairs were straight ahead, a blue parlor with an oriental rug was to the right, and the dining room, which had a doorway that he assumed led to the kitchen, was to the left.

Gwen removed her hat pin and placed her hat on a coatrack next to the door before stating, "It's almost suppertime. She's probably cooking."

They went past the long, sturdy pine table and chairs through the opening into the kitchen. A middle-aged woman with a droopy, graying brown bun was removing a pan of corn bread from the wood-burning stove.

"I'm back," Gwen announced lightly.

"Glad to hear it." Mrs. Brown gave Gwen a motherly smile. "We're just about ready to eat."

"You know I'm always ready for a good meal," Gwen joked. She touched Josh's sleeve and pulled him forward. "Mrs. Brown, this is an old friend of mine, Josh Flynn."

They exchanged greetings and Gwen hurried on, "Mrs. Brown, Josh is moving to Shawnee to work at the Rock Island shops, and I know you don't normally rent to men, but Mr. Vance's apartment has been vacant for a long time and I can vouch for Josh's character." She stopped to take a breath.

Josh grinned at Gwen's valiant effort. "She's right, ma'am. Never a truer gentleman will you find."

"A railroad man, huh? I don't know…" Mrs. Brown appeared to be considering the possibility.

"I'll be handy to have around. I can fix most anything, and I'll be a strong back to haul firewood and the like," he added.

"He's a carpenter. Weren't there some porch steps that needed to be replaced and a door upstairs that needed repair?" Gwen asked.

"That's true…"

"He could use the carriage house for his carpentry work. I'll help him organize all the things stored in there," Gwen reassured her.

"All right, Mr. Flynn. Gwen is a good talker. I'll give you a try." Mrs. Brown pointed to a closed door at the rear of the house. "You can use that bathroom there. The one upstairs is for the ladies only. And there shouldn't ever be any reason for you to be up there. If I find out you have been, it'll mean immediate eviction." She gave him a stern look.

"Of course, ma'am."

She went to a set of metal hooks by the back door and took down a skeleton key. "Go see what you think about the place. If it suits you, I'll have water on to boil for cleaning it up after supper."

"Thank you, ma'am." He took the key from her and shook her hand.

He and Gwen went out onto the small porch. They had to step over a couple of rotten boards as they walked to the carriage house in the southwest corner of the big backyard. They climbed the stairs up the side of the building. The exterior was in need of a new coat of white paint, but it seemed sound. There were no wobbly railings or rickety steps. They paused on the landing, which was large enough for a chair, to enjoy the evenings. He inserted the key and unlocked the door. It protested with a loud squeak as he pushed it open.

"Oh good, it doesn't smell as if mice have taken up residence," Gwen commented as she entered. "There's an old tomcat that prowls around. He must be a good mouser. It is a bit stuffy, though." She flung open the uncovered window near the door. The window facing the street was a bit more stubborn, but after struggling with it, she gave a shout of success.

As the cross breeze began to air out the place, Josh took stock of his prospective home. Though dusty and riddled with cobwebs, it had potential. It was a nice-sized room with a simple dark maple bedroom set. The bed was in the far right corner. A wood-burning stove was on the wall opposite the door. There was a chest of drawers, an old wardrobe, and a washstand with a blue-and-white pitcher and basin. A small, square oak table and chairs were at the other end of the room along with a short walnut bookshelf.

"What do you think?" Gwen asked as she turned to him with her hands on her hips.

"It'll need a fair bit of cleaning," he noted.

"We'll get it done."

"Let me see if the space downstairs will work," he said. He thought he should check it all out before he committed fully, but in his heart, he knew it would take wild horses to drag him away.

"Of course."

She smiled on her way out the door. He marveled at how captivating she was. Yet he could tell by her demeanor that she was humble and not vain at all.

Downstairs, in the front of the carriage house, he lifted the simple latch, grabbed the handle on each door, and tugged. At first unyielding, the doors finally scraped the rust-colored dirt as he yanked them open.

The dim interior brightened as the doors were opened. Two small windows were along the west wall on the opposite side and a single window hung on the south side and north side. As his eyes adjusted to the gloom, he noticed furniture in various stages of disrepair, old trunks, a two-seated bicycle, garden tools, and other miscellaneous things scattered about. Dust rose from the dirt floor as he shuffled around. Under the double windows, he spotted an old workbench that was piled with crates and had a vise at one end. He reached out and shook it. It wasn't too rickety. A couple of braces underneath would fix it right up.

"So?" Gwen peered at him expectantly.

"It'll do." He nodded.

"Good." She clapped her hands and grinned. "Let's go in and tell Mrs. Brown."

"Let's," he agreed.

Gwen all but skipped toward the house. She was more mature and womanly than the girl he had known, yet she was still as carefree as he remembered. He was more than impressed with her.

She leaned toward him and said in hushed tones, "There are three other boarders here." She held up two fingers. "Marie Petricek and Liza Ast are best friends that moved in about the same time. Marie is the tall, thin one with brown hair. Liza is the shorter one with black hair. Both are sweet girls. Bevin Brody moved in a couple of weeks ago. She seems nice. She has strawberry blonde hair and a sprinkling of freckles across her nose. If I remember correctly, her family was originally from Dublin, Ireland, and she has the most amazing blue eyes I've ever seen. They're how I imagine the ocean looks. You can almost see through them."

"That's quite observant of you," he commented as he smiled down at her.

"Oh..." She flapped her hand in dismissal. "Since I like to write, I like to observe people."

"That reminds me of a game we used to play. Remember when we would sit on my porch steps and watch shoppers go into Mr. Frank's store?"

"Yes! I loved that game!" She stopped and squeezed his arm in excitement. "One of us would pick out the person's distinguishing feature and the other would have to guess what it was."

"I believe I won the most often," he said smugly.

She gave an unladylike snort. "Well, only you would notice knitting needles poking out of a man's suit coat pocket or the bare feet of a fancy-dressed lady."

"I beg to differ." He tapped his temple. "'Tis a keen eye I have." He chuckled as he remembered how often she used to complain about him winning.

"Fine. Fine. I see I'm not going to win this argument either." She rolled her eyes, but her smile belied her amusement.

They entered the warm, delectable-smelling kitchen. He removed his jacket and hat, placing them on hooks by the door. Gwen had begun washing up at the sink. Their skin touched as she handed him the bar of lye soap. He wondered if she felt the same thrill run up her arm from the slippery contact. He bent his head and scrubbed while she rinsed her long fingers.

Mrs. Brown bustled in and picked up a coffeepot and a crockery pitcher full of milk. "What's your opinion, Mr. Flynn?" Mrs. Brown asked with raised eyebrows.

"I'll take it."

"That's fine and dandy. Join us fer supper. We'll take care of cleaning the place up after our bellies are full."

In the dining room, the other boarders, all as Gwen had described, were waiting patiently in their seats. After holding the chair for a surprised Mrs. Brown at the head of the table, Josh walked past the two young women he assumed were Liza and Bevin to get the chair for Gwen, next to Marie. When Gwen was settled, he took the chair at the end next to her.

The blessing was said and platters and bowls were passed around. He piled his plate with brown beans, fried potatoes, tomato relish, and yellow corn bread.

"Mr. Flynn is going to be our new boarder," Mrs. Brown announced as she put a slice of onion on her plate. "He'll live out back."

All hues of pretty eyes turned his way with interest.

Miss Brody gave him a sidelong glance. "What brings you here, Mr. Flynn?" she asked with an obvious Dublin lilt to her voice.

"As me own sainted grandmother used to say, ''Tis the work that put the wind in me sails and put me feet to travel,'" he mused, exaggerating his own accent as he liked to do when it fancied him.

"What he's trying to say is that he has transferred in to the Rock Island." Gwen snickered.

Miss Brody gave him a genuine smile. "'Tis glad we are that you're joining us."

He could have sworn he saw a hint of suspicion from Gwen when she glanced at Miss Brody before returning her eyes to her plate. But when she dug into her food as if nothing bothered her, he thought he must have been mistaken.

CHAPTER THREE

Josh had never seen such a flurry of activity. After supper, everyone in the house offered to help clean his new home. They donned their work aprons and went to the carriage house with brooms, mops, buckets, and rags in tow. He was amazed and slightly humbled to receive such enthusiastic help. That he was surrounded by some of the bonniest creatures in Oklahoma Territory only made the evening more enjoyable.

After moving furniture so the fair young maidens could clean the carriage house, he was told by Mrs. Brown to take the sheet-covered mattress off of his new bed so it could be dusted. By the time he hefted the mattress to the back porch and unwrapped it, his helpers were descending the stairs of the carriage house with their tools in hand. He thanked them with a formal bow as Mrs. Brown began whacking the mattress with a rug beater. Luckily it wasn't too dusty. Mrs. Brown gave it a good pounding anyway.

Marie, Liza, and Bevin, who insisted they all be on a first-name basis, bid him good night. Just then Gwen emerged with an armload of fresh linens.

Mrs. Brown sighed as she straightened from her task. "I'll get you set up in no time." She started to take the linens from Gwen.

"I don't mind finishing it up, Mrs. Brown," Gwen offered. "You can go on and get the supper dishes done."

The older woman nodded but gave Gwen a stern glare. "Keep the door open and don't lollygag. And there should be no reason for you to be up there any other time either."

"I'm engaged, Mrs. Brown," Gwen said, as if that was enough of an explanation.

"I don't want no inappropriate behavior around here."

"There's no need to worry about me," Gwen assured her.

"All right, missy." She gave Gwen a friendly swat on the backside with the rug beater. "Better see to it."

"Yes, ma'am." Gwen scooted past the landlady with a dangerous weapon.

Josh grinned as he picked up the mattress again. He had to admit that he was a tad affronted that Gwen thought him so harmless. If she only knew how often he had dreamed of holding her in his arms if he ever found her, she might not be so cavalier. But then, she *was* engaged to be married, and that meant he had to somehow put all thoughts like that aside.

They entered his new flat, now sparkling clean and smelling like soap. He dropped the mattress on the bed frame. Gwen handed him part of her load. "I'll hang the curtains. You can work on the sheets," she informed him.

She stood on a chair, took down the rod, and began to insert it into the green plaid curtains while he started making the bed.

"On the train, we were so busy talking about my job and some of the people I've interviewed I forgot to ask you about your family. They're all well?" Gwen asked.

"They are. My parents are grand. My brothers and sisters are all married with children, even wee Beth."

"Beth? Why, she was just a girl when I saw her last." She shook her head in amazement. "And your grandparents? Granny Riley?"

Both sets of his grandparents, who had made the voyage from Ireland during the famine, had been alive when he had last seen

Gwen. The elder Flynns had stayed in Kansas City when his parents ventured down to Guthrie for carpentry work in the new city. His maternal grandmother, Granny Riley, had lived with his family for as long as he could remember. "They're all gone now. Granny Riley died about a year ago."

His granny had been quite a force in his life. All five feet of her had been full of spunk, humor, and advice. Just before she died, she told him that all the young women he had chased over the years had only been a shadow of the girl he had loved when he was a boy. She told him he would never be happy unless he found Gwen again and put her memory behind him once and for all.

"I'm sorry, Josh. She was a corker," she said sympathetically before moving the chair to the other window.

"Aye. That she was." He smiled sadly. "How's your family?"

"Great. Pa is still with the surveying crew for the Santa Fe. He's not home much. Mother is still Mother. Prim and proper as usual. My two younger brothers, George and Gilbert, are thirteen."

"Really? That's amazing."

He remembered how distant and distraught her mother had been when he knew them. She had moved her family to Guthrie after the deaths of Gwen's younger brother and sister from a tornado on their farm.

He adjusted the sheets on the bed until they were reasonably straight and shook out a white bedspread. Gwen stepped down from the second window and came to help him.

"What about your man?" He ventured to ask about the person who had won her heart.

"My man?" She furrowed her brows. "Oh, you mean Walter. Walter Manning. He's a lawyer in Guthrie."

"So when is the happy day?"

"The last Saturday in November." She gave him a quiet smile.

It wasn't exactly the glowing reaction he had expected from a soon-to-be-married woman. It made him wonder. He quickly realized it was probably only wishful speculation on his part.

"What about you? You've been able to resist the charms of the ladies?"

"I was nearly snared last year, but I escaped by the hair on me chin," he jested.

He'd had his fair share of dalliances in the past, but the last one, Susannah Nelson, was his one regret. He had enjoyed the company of the dark-haired beauty immensely. When she began to talk about marriage, he didn't think much about it, but after his granny died, he panicked. Susannah wasn't the love of his life. He tried to be as gentle as he could when he told her good-bye, but he knew she harbored hard feelings against him.

"You weren't ready to settle down?" she asked.

His thoughts came back to the present. He examined her inquisitive eyes and her lovely face. "She just wasn't the one."

"So you're one of those who believe a person only has one true love?"

"I'm no philosopher, so I couldn't say. But I do know when I find her there'll be no stopping me until she's mine." He thought he saw disbelief in her expression. He crossed his arms and inquired, "What is your opinion on the matter?"

She seemed to squirm a mite before she finally waved her hand. "Oh, I don't know. I figure we marry who best suits us."

"That's not a very romantic notion coming from a young woman," he couldn't resist remarking.

"It's the practical side of me." She shrugged.

"I used to know a girl who was full of wonder and dreams."

She almost appeared hurt before she replied curtly, "We must all grow up, mustn't we?" She moved to the door. "I'll help you bring your trunk up if you'd like."

He felt bad that he had spoken so freely and put a damper on such a wondrous day. "I'd appreciate it." He put his hand amiably on her shoulder. "I'm glad I found my old friend again. I've thought of you many times over the years."

"You have?" She appeared to be trying to decide what to say. She suddenly grinned mischievously. "I'd bet a ladies' man like you never gave a childhood friend like me another thought."

"Not true. Not true." He wagged his head. "When an angry father would find me hiding behind his fence or bushes, I'd think of me old chum Gwen and wish she were there with her gift of the gab to talk me way out. Instead, I became the fastest runner in Wyandotte County."

She laughed. "I thought you looked rather fit." She headed for the door. "Now we'd better get that trunk or Mrs. Brown will never trust us."

~

It was just about dark by the time Josh had unloaded his belongings. He had placed his clothing in the wardrobe and the chest of drawers and put his hats on top of the chest. He left the trunk at the foot of his bed with his carpentry tools still inside. It had taken a long time to collect all the chisels, saws, planes, and everything else. He would store them in there for now instead of taking them downstairs. He liked to have a place to keep them safe.

He pulled the chain to the single light bulb in the center of the ceiling. He was glad electricity had been run to the carriage house when the previous tenant lived there.

Too invigorated to even think about going to sleep yet, he grabbed a chair so he could sit on the porch. He opened the door, and his nose was inches away from Gwen's knuckles, about to knock. They both gave a surprised chuckle. He put the chair down.

"Mrs. Brown thought you might like an extra light." She handed him a kerosene lamp and some matches.

"Tell her many thanks."

"I will." She stood there awkwardly for a moment before her eyes met his. "Mass is at ten o'clock in the morning. Marie, Liza, and I usually walk to church together. You're welcome to join us, if you'd like."

"I would." He nodded.

"Good…well…have a good night," Gwen said before she hurried down the stairs.

He stood there long after she had departed. He was all in a muddle about Gwen Sanders. She was almost as he had imagined after all these years, but he was confused by her behavior. She was at times genuinely friendly, aloof at others, and, like now, almost shy. He didn't know what to think about her. All he did know was that his gut hurt to think she loved another man.

He needed some kind of revelation. Should he stay or go? He didn't want to fall for her and torture himself, but he couldn't see moving away from her either. He supposed his only option for now was to keep put and decide as time went on what he should do.

He sighed, and as he turned to put the lantern away, he noticed a light shining from an upstairs window in the house. He paused to see if it was Gwen's room. Before long, he viewed Bevin walking past the window, brushing her long golden-red hair. He thought she caught sight of him before she pulled the shade down.

He let out a low whistle and shook his head as he went in. Bevin was a beauty, but he wasn't interested. No one could hold a candle to Gwen.

Who knew how his life would turn out? He certainly didn't. He guessed he was ready to find out.

CHAPTER FOUR

Gwen was irritated. She was going to be late again if she didn't hurry. Marie had knocked on her bedroom door about ten minutes before and said she and Liza were going on to the church without her.

She jammed on a fancy black straw hat festooned with ivory muslin roses and loops of brown and black ribbons and poked the long pin through, securing it dubiously. It would probably be prudent to do it again, but she didn't have time. She donned the Eton-style jacket to her amber-colored taffeta silk suit. It was a new suit with a double-breasted jacket reaching a trifle below the waistline of the flounced skirt. She had been trying to build up a respectable trousseau so she would make Walter proud. This was one of the first outfits she had purchased, and she liked the cut of it.

She grabbed her black kid gloves and brown leather bag before rushing out the door. Her polished black boots clattered as she sped down the stairs. She wished she had made her appearance in a slightly more dignified manner when she spotted Josh rising from the sofa in the parlor.

Josh walked toward her and grinned. Whether it was from amusement at her entrance or because he was glad to see her she couldn't decipher. Her cousin, Luke, used to tease her about her unladylike behavior. She knew he was only joking, but she did hope she could begin to show a little more decorum.

She was slightly taken aback by how dashing Josh looked. He was wearing a brown suit that had occasional tan threads throughout. There was a splash of dark red in the brown paisley-patterned silk necktie that encircled a tall, stiff, white linen collar. His brown fedora with a red band was perched jauntily on his head. She was temporarily speechless, which was entirely unusual for her.

"Do I look respectable enough?" he asked with a gleam in his eye.

She hoped her jaw hadn't dropped while she was taking in the sight of him. She finally got her mouth to work. "Of course," she said as she flapped her hand. "We'd better go."

She wondered how unbecoming it would be showing up at church with such an attractive escort to whom she wasn't related or married. If she had gone with Marie and Liza as planned, there would have been no impropriety arriving with a group. She didn't have time to ponder it now, though. They would be late for sure.

She hurried forward and almost collided with Josh as he hastened to open the door for her. They both mumbled apologies as he closed it behind them.

"You look…stunning…if I'm allowed to say so," he said softly.

She glanced at him to see if he was serious. He appeared to be. "Thank you," she mumbled. She ducked her head and headed down the walkway at a little less than a trot. His long strides matched hers easily. She put her bag on her arm and worked at pulling her gloves on while they walked.

"I figured you'd gone ahead with the others," she stated as she buttoned the left glove.

"I was definitely tempted to have a leisurely stroll with such beauties, but—"

"But you decided to have a mad dash with your old chum instead," she interjected.

"Of course. Who wouldn't?" He chuckled and patted his chest. "It's good for the constitution."

"Oh, drat," she muttered. "I always have trouble getting this one buttoned." She paused at the corner of Tenth and Market while she struggled with her other glove.

"Let me," he offered. His fingers were slender yet strong and nimble, and he completed the task quickly. His hands were sinewy and the raised blue veins on the backs indicated he made his living working with them.

"Thanks," she said quietly as she removed her hand from his. She wished she hadn't noticed his hands. Walter's thick, blunt fingers had never inspired admiration in her writer's mind. She did not like that realization. She was happy that Josh was a friend again, but she should not begin to compare him to Walter. There was no reason to do so.

"Let's move on," she remarked quickly. She looked both ways before crossing the brick-paved street. "We have several blocks to go."

They resumed their brisk pace, not leaving much room for idle conversation. At last the nearly completed redbrick church was in view. Scaffolding surrounded the steeply pitched slate roofline and the tall bell tower. The church dwarfed the three-storied rectory to the west.

"Now that's a grand cathedral." Josh was noticeably impressed.

"It's supposed to seat at least seven hundred. The dedication is next month. Hopefully it'll all be finished by then." She trudged on, trying to catch her breath. "We're still using the old church nearby."

They came up to the white clapboard church with a few other parishioners. They went up the wooden steps and entered the small vestibule. The large room contained rows of pews and a curtain toward the front that was pulled back, which separated the altar from the rest of the room during the week so the nuns could run their school.

Gwen spotted her best friend, Rose Emerson, with her new husband and step-baby sitting next to her cousin Luke and his wife, Ada, but there weren't any free spaces near them. She led the way toward one of the few spots remaining up front, in plain view of everyone. She hoped the congregation would pay more attention to Father Schneider than whom she was sitting with.

She was afraid to say she fretted most of the time instead of actively participating. She tried not to stand too close to Josh when he held the hymnal for her but still noticed his excellent tenor singing voice. Music wasn't important to Walter and he wouldn't even mouth the words to songs. She didn't dare show the appreciation she felt for Josh's singing.

It was quite a relief when the hour was over and the parishioners departed. Gwen wanted to make a quick escape, but she found that impossible. Rose, Owen, and Mrs. Dennis, who was holding baby Hope, approached them as soon as they stepped onto the grass outside.

Rose gave Gwen a sweet smile, a questioning look in her blue eyes.

"Gwen. It's nice to see you have returned," Mrs. Dennis greeted. "This must be your young man." She nodded to Josh. "We missed you at Rose's wedding."

Gwen didn't know what bothered her more, remembering that Walter had been too busy to come to her best friend's wedding or that Mrs. Dennis assumed that Josh was Walter.

Rose, obviously appalled by her mother's mistake, said quickly, "No, Mother, this isn't Walter."

Mrs. Dennis was noticeably chagrined. "I'm sorry, dear."

"It's fine, Mrs. Dennis. You couldn't know." Gwen motioned to Josh. "This is Josh Flynn. He's an old friend of the family. He just moved to Shawnee, and I'm showing him around."

Owen leaned forward, and a light-brown curl fell onto his forehead from his combed-back hair. He had a ready smile and extended a hand to Josh. "Any friend of Gwen's is a friend of ours."

Luke and Ada emerged from the crowd and came up to them. Ada was in the late stages of pregnancy, but was still the most captivating woman alive. Ada's emerald eyes sparkled with curiosity as Gwen introduced Josh to them.

"I was tellin' Ada you looked familiar. Flynn? Flynn." Luke's brown eyes squinted as he tried to remember. He pushed up his Sunday bowler hat and scratched his head, making his hair spiky. "Flynn. You lived next to Gwen for a while, didn't you? Am I right?" Luke asked.

"Aye, that'd be me." Josh smiled as he shook Luke's hand.

"We had a fine time, didn't we? I'll never forget the man who taught me to roller-skate. I was black-and-blue by the time I learned, but I was determined to not let Gwen's sweetheart beat me at anything." Luke laughed.

"We were just friends," Gwen informed him.

"You know how to roller-skate?" Ada looked up at Luke with a mixture of amusement and admiration.

"I surely do. Just one more talent your husband has," he joked as he winked at Ada. He turned back to Josh, put his arm amiably over his shoulders, and asked as they walked off with Ada toward Luke's carriage, "You moved away years ago, didn't you? What brings you back to Oklahoma Territory?"

Rose placed her hand on Gwen's forearm as the others walked away. "Ada and Luke are coming over for lunch. You and Josh will join us, won't you?"

"I can. Josh would probably prefer to eat at Mrs. Brown's." Rose's curious eyes turned in her direction. "He's renting Mr. Vance's old room over the carriage house."

They all nodded but didn't speak. Gwen wondered what they were thinking.

Suddenly Luke turned back and shouted, "Rose, would you mind if we have another for lunch? Josh and I'd like to talk over old times."

"Yes. Of course he can join us," she answered.

Gwen hoped she didn't look as nervous as she felt.

"You can ride with us." Owen offered an arm, and Gwen took his elbow as Rose held onto his other arm.

They strolled to Owen's fringe-topped surrey. He helped Gwen and Rose into the plush green leather seats in the back while he assisted his mother-in-law and Hope into the front seat. He climbed in, picked up the reins, released the brake, and urged the bay horse on.

Rose leaned toward Gwen, the brims of their hats touching, and whispered, "You don't seem particularly thrilled to have Josh around. Is he not as he appears?"

Gwen listened to the clip-clop of the horse's hooves for a moment before she let out a long, low sigh. She knew she could confide in her best friend. "No, that's not it. He was the one I told you about last fall. I used to sit at my window and watch for him from my upstairs room. I'd wait for him to come like he said he would when I had to move away." The breeze was cool on her face. She brushed a stray hair away. "He seems as fun and genuine as when we were young. I just…"

"Are you afraid those old fanciful feelings might return?" Rose asked sympathetically.

"Oh no." She was shocked. "That's not it. I love Walter. We've even set the date for the last Saturday in November."

"Oh…" Rose blushed. "Congratulations."

"Thank you." Gwen took a deep breath and related her fears. "What I'm afraid of is that people will *assume* we are a couple just as your mother did. That would cause such a scandal…I'm almost scared to be nice to him because I'm worried what others will think."

"I didn't know things like that troubled you." Rose took her hand and patted it.

Gwen grimaced. "Well, when I'm working, I try to appear fearless, but I fret and stew over everyone's opinions. My mother used to stress that we needed to be virtuous women, and she would say strength and honor are our clothing. So I've always tried to live honorably and not do anything that even *seemed* shameful. The most daring thing I ever did was move here, and I wouldn't have done that if Walter and Mama had thought it was disgraceful."

Rose nodded and seemed to be in deep thought. "I would hate for you not to be your usual jovial self. I don't believe it would be indecent if you were amiable with an old friend."

A smile slowly crept onto Gwen's face. "Well, you're the most decent person I know, and if you think so, then I won't worry about it."

CHAPTER FIVE

"So tell me more about Gwen's escapades while I was away workin' on that ranch," Luke said from the front seat of his buggy.

Mrs. Logan, or Ada, as she insisted, gave Josh a friendly smile as she glanced back at him from the front seat. He hadn't been around many women who were expecting, but he had never seen a prettier mother-to-be.

"Did she ever tell you about the time we climbed up to the roof of Mr. Frank's store and then hopped from roof to roof? She would grab her skirts and take a running leap with braids flying. We had gone probably half a block before we were spotted," Josh remembered fondly.

Ada appeared startled and Luke gave a surprised chuckle. "I bet Aunt Grace wasn't any too happy about that."

"No." He laughed. "We had been in a few fair scraps, but I do believe that was the final blow." He shook his head at the memory of Mrs. Sanders giving them both her sternest lecture. "We weren't allowed out of our yards together after that. We still had a good time, though. My old mates used to wonder why I liked spending so much time with a girl, but who wouldn't want to play with someone who was as bold as a lad *and* lovely to look at?"

"I know what you mean. I'd rather look at a pretty face any day." Luke nodded toward his wife before he pulled up on the reins. "We're here," he stated.

The buggy stopped behind the Emersons' surrey. The occupants had already departed and were stepping onto the porch of the Emersons' large white two-story house with dark-red trim. Josh sought out Gwen. She was laughing and seemed lighthearted. Maybe her strange mood had lifted. She had been a little aloof this morning.

He hopped down as Luke assisted his wife. He sauntered up the walkway and entered with them.

Ahead was a wide, elegant staircase. The varnished pine floor led into the parlor that was sparsely yet comfortably furnished. A large fireplace with an ornate oak mantel was on one side of the room while an upright piano was prominently featured on the opposite wall. He followed his hosts into a spacious dining room with tall oak wainscoting. A row of four big windows looked out onto a porch and a nicely sized backyard.

The ladies began to remove their hats and gloves.

"I thought we would have a breakfast with sausage, eggs, biscuits, and gravy. How does that sound?" Rose asked.

Enthusiastic murmurs of agreement came from everyone.

"I thought I'd try my hand at baking scones, if you don't mind?" Gwen asked Rose.

"Of course I don't mind. It sounds wonderful," Rose agreed. "Do you need to find a recipe?"

Gwen gazed at Josh for a moment. There was a twinkle in her eyes. "No. I believe I remember the ingredients."

Josh had a warm feeling inside as the ladies walked away. The vision of Granny Riley teaching flour-covered Gwen how to make scones flitted into his mind. He had enjoyed sitting at the table and watching as flour dust floated in the sunlight from the window while Gwen concentrated on her work. He had even eaten the rock-hard attempts before she finally accomplished making them as light as air.

The men made small talk while the ladies cooked. Josh told them about himself and his work. He found out that Owen Emerson ran a store in town called B & B Mercantile and that Luke had some cattle and a few horses and was going to try his hand at raising some wheat.

Gwen emerged from the kitchen carrying a stack of dishes. She began to place the red-and-white floral plates on the table. She was humming a tune as she glanced up from her task. Her joyful smile caught Josh off guard. Was he the sole recipient of such favors? He saw the other two men still conversing. He grinned back at her and was comforted that she continued to smile instead of running away.

~

Gwen reached for the homemade apple jelly to put on her fluffy scone. The meal was about to end, but she wasn't quite full yet. She really enjoyed sitting around the table with good food and company. She wondered how many more times she would get to experience it before she had to move back to Guthrie. She couldn't think of it now, though, or it would make her gloomy.

"I just have to say again how good these scones are, Gwen. I don't believe I've ever had any. They're mighty tasty," Luke commented before popping a butter-covered bite into his mouth.

"I had a patient teacher a long time ago," Gwen remarked.

Josh looked pleased. "Granny Riley would be proud."

Gwen felt a blush creep up into her cheeks from his compliment.

"Who was Granny Riley?" Ada asked as she took a sip of coffee.

Gwen was relieved to turn her thoughts to something else. "She was Josh's grandmother, but she was like one to me. She would tell stories from Ireland and tell of her adventures coming to America. She taught me how to make soda bread, barm brack, and a potato dish called boxty." Gwen grinned. "She even told me a little rhyme, 'Boxty on the griddle, boxty in the pan, if you can't make boxty, you'll never get your man.'"

Ada chuckled. "So did making boxty help you snare Walter?"

Gwen was taken aback by the question, but tried to smile to cover her reaction. "Oh no, it was my charms alone," she joked. She couldn't tell them that Walter would probably be appalled if she cooked him Irish peasant food.

Josh studied Gwen a tad too long for her comfort. His lips were upturned with mirth, but there was something lurking in the depths of his dark eyes. Looking away, she fidgeted with her napkin.

Josh turned his attention to the other people at the table. "Gwen's easy manner has charmed the lads for years. And I for one appreciate her friendship. I also want to thank all of you for the kindly way you have received me. You've made a stranger welcome." He held up his teacup for a toast.

Luke lifted his coffee cup. "To friends—old and new."

Everybody raised their glasses and there were smiles all around. "To friends."

Gwen was privately thrilled. She didn't know why it mattered so much that her friends, and especially Luke, should like Josh, but it did. Josh's eye caught hers and she ducked her head.

"I'll gather the dishes if you're all finished," Gwen offered.

"I'll help you," Ada said.

"I can get it."

"I need to move around anyway." Ada pushed her large form up from her chair, still managing to appear graceful. She picked up her plate and Luke's.

"I'll take Hope upstairs for her nap," Mrs. Dennis noted as she carried out the eighteen-month-old.

"Thank you, Mother," Rose called after her.

Gwen and Ada followed Rose into the bright-yellow kitchen. Ada deposited her dishes into the sink and put a hand to her back.

"I just can't seem to get comfortable these days." She sighed. Slight smudges of blue under her eyes were the only sign of the discomfort she must be feeling. "I can't sit for long or stand for any time. Sleeping is a feat of its own. My back aches terribly."

"I'm sorry for your troubles," Rose comforted.

"Thank you. But I know I'm not the first woman to go through this. I'm reassured knowing it will be over before too long." Ada placed her hand lightly on her extended form. "This will probably be the last time I come to town, though. The buggy ride was torturous this morning."

"That's a shame." Gwen patted Ada's arm.

"I want you two to promise to come out and see me. I'll perish from loneliness if you don't visit." Ada's lips turned up.

"Of course we will," Rose remarked.

"All you have to do is tell us the day," Gwen agreed.

"How about a May Day celebration? It will be a final hurrah before the baby is born."

"Sounds wonderful. Just don't put yourself out any," Gwen said.

"Yes. We'll bring the food. We don't want you standing in front of a hot stove on our account," Rose added.

Ada laughed. "I don't think you'd want me at the stove for another reason, but if you insist—"

"We do!" Rose and Gwen said in unison and chuckled with her.

"Invite Walter too," Ada said.

"I will, but I'd be surprised if he could come. His work takes up an awful lot of his time." Gwen shrugged.

Ada nodded sympathetically. "Well, tell Josh he's welcome. He seems a rather likable fellow."

"Yes. He is," Gwen acknowledged. "I've had fond memories of him all these years. It's nice to see he hasn't changed for the worse."

"So how *did* he return into your life?" Ada leaned as close as her body would allow, her elegant eyebrows arched with curiosity.

"Now *that* is an amazing story." Gwen crossed her arms and settled against the icebox to tell the tale.

～

That evening, Josh leaned back in his chair and put his feet up on the railing of his little porch. It was almost too dark to whittle, but he dug his pocketknife out of his trousers so he could work on a six-by-six-inch piece of cedar that he had found. He wasn't sure what he would make yet. A lot of times he didn't know on smaller pieces until he could get a feel for the grain and how it could be carved.

He flicked open his knife and ran the sharp blade along the length of the block. The first few shavings emitted the pungent odor. That was one of the things he liked most about working with wood. Cedar had its definite smell, so did pine and other species.

He continued carving while he thought about his day. He had been glad to meet Gwen's comrades and visit with them. It was quite a relief knowing that Gwen had grown into a confident, fun young woman and surrounded herself with people of quality. He hoped he could be counted as one now.

A terrible commotion in the bushes at the back of the yard caught his attention. He'd never heard such a racket of caterwauling and hissing. Finally a small gray cat dashed out of the bushes, running for safety as fast as it could. At length, a huge orange male cat strutted out and sat down to groom himself. He had a ragged ear, scruffy fur, and one eye that was blue. He definitely was not a handsome fellow.

"Got him out of your territory, eh?" Josh asked the cat.

The cat gave him a wary glare.

"So you were the one that kept me up most of last night screeching like a banshee."

The tomcat ignored him and went about his business.

"Not very friendly are you, you old son of a goat?" Josh smirked. "*Mac gabhair*...if my Irish doesn't fail me."

The cat finally stared up at Josh as if it wondered why he was still talking.

"Mac. That's what I'll call you." He pointed the knife at him. "I wonder, Mac, if I could run off Mr. Walter Manning the way you chased that fellow away?" He sighed. "But no, you're a cat, and I'm supposed to be a gentleman. I can't bully people around. 'Tis a pity, though. I can't shake the feeling that he's not right for Gwen."

Mac stood, stretched his full length with toes spread. He straightened up, twitched his tail, turned his back on Josh, and sauntered off.

"Nice talkin' to you," Josh muttered with a smile.

CHAPTER SIX

Monday morning Gwen arrived at the *Shawnee Globe* on Broadway, north of the Norwood Hotel. She glanced at her attire in her reflection in the glass of the door. She was wearing what she considered her most professional outfit: a gray wool walking skirt, crisp white shirtwaist with a little puff at the shoulders, stiff linen collar, and a black silk necktie. Her flat-topped straw hat with a black band of ribbon was set at an angle.

She pulled open the door to the newspaper office. The odor of pipe and cigar smoke mingled with printer's ink and filled her nostrils even before she took a step inside. The small ocher-colored room was cramped with four desks. The largest one, at the far right, belonged to the editor, Mr. Jennings. There was an aisle just wide enough for her to navigate past the desks of Mr. Spitzer and Mr. Abrams.

"Good morning!" she said cheerily.

Mr. Spitzer gave her a nod as he took a long draw on his pipe. Mr. Abrams pushed his spectacles farther up his nose as he glanced up at her before he continued to scratch on a piece of paper with his pen.

She had to admit, it was a burr under her saddle that the men here weren't friendlier. She never felt outright animosity from them, but she usually had the feeling they were only humoring her. Since she wanted people to like her, it was difficult to work in such an environment. She had to keep reminding herself that this was all temporary and she was only working here to hone her writing skills so she could write that novel.

She passed her small desk, which was little more than a wobbly table, and went straight to Mr. Jennings. Her boss was a balding gentleman with light hair who was on the portly side and usually red of face. His complexion wasn't ruddy because he was an excitable man. The contrary was true. He was even-keeled and tried to run his business as smoothly as possible.

"Here's my article on the most recent dinner the ladies from St. Benedict's had for a church fund-raiser," she informed him as she handed him the handwritten page.

"Good." He placed it on the top tray at the left edge of his desk. He looked up at her. "I have something I'd like you to cover."

"Yes?"

"Katie Barnard, that young lady that's running for the state's first commissioner of charities and corrections, is going to be speaking tomorrow to some union labor people. She'll be at Woodland Park at six thirty. I'd like you to go and write an article about it."

"Yes, sir," she accepted excitedly as she turned away.

This would be her first real piece for the paper. Not that she minded writing about the arts and the society folk of Shawnee, but to write about the first woman who was involved in the new state's politics was a privilege.

Kate Barnard had organized quite a bit of charity work in Oklahoma City and had made a name for herself by helping to get anti-child-labor laws included in Oklahoma's constitution. Back in December, she had spoken at the constitutional convention in Guthrie for those provisions. Gwen had read about it in the Guthrie paper and had admired Miss Barnard's pluck and determination.

It wasn't until she sat down at her desk that she realized she had probably received the assignment because the men hadn't thought it was important enough. Oh well, she sighed inwardly. Why should she second-guess everything? It was their loss if they thought so. She just needed to take the assignment at face value and do an excellent job.

～

Josh stepped over the rails of one of the many sets of tracks in the Rock Island Lines yard and shops. The pungent odor of creosote hung in the air as he stepped on a railroad tie. The smell didn't bother him as it did some. He almost liked it. It always brought back memories of when he was a lad and watched the gigantic steam engines pass by.

The yard was a huge maze of tracks, trains, and redbrick buildings at the west end of Main Street on the southern side. The freight car repair shop, foundry with billowing smokestacks, curved roundhouse and turntable, and lumber mill were scattered around the yard. His building, the coach repair shop, was to the east of the freight car shop.

Ballast crunched under his worn but newly polished work boots as he made his way across all the tracks, being mindful of engines that might approach at any moment. As he neared his building, he brushed a white thread off his denim trousers, straightened the lay-down collar on his light-blue cotton shirt, and adjusted the strap on one of his blue-and-white striped suspenders.

He walked through the door that was propped open. The coach repair shop was a long, spacious structure. A dismantled coach sat there, and men were doing their various jobs around the place. A few men glanced his way before returning to their tasks.

Luckily a supervisor had shown him around when he had come down from Kansas for the interview. He headed straight for the stairs and went up the narrow passageway. The expansive second floor held the upholstery shop and cabinet shop. Dye vats, hair and moss storage bins, a cutting bench, and various other racks and vats were at one end of the building while saws, sanders, and other machines hummed on the other side. All the equipment was run by a large belt-and-shaft system, with the belts coming up from the first floor.

An older man with a head full of gray hair looked up from the plank he was putting a mortise in. He came to Josh with a hand extended.

"Hi, there. I'm J. D. Miller. You must be the new fella."

"Yes, Josh Flynn's the name."

Miller gave a wide sweep of an arm. "This is my crew."

Some of the men looked up and smiled while others ignored them. There were seven or so workers in the department.

"Sorry I'm late. It took longer to walk here than I thought," Josh apologized.

"It's all right, since it's your first day. Just don't let it happen again," Miller said sternly, but there was a twinkle of understanding in his eye. He pointed to the far wall. "That's Chuck Thompson over there. Your bench is next to his. He'll show you the ropes for the next few days."

"Yes, sir." Josh tipped his hat. He shuffled through wood shavings and sawdust to his new work area.

He introduced himself to Thompson, who only grunted in return. Thompson was younger and shorter than himself with dingy blond hair that was slicked back.

"Put that table together," Thompson instructed without any cordiality about it.

"Surely." Josh looked through the stack of lumber that was piled on the bench and began to sort the pieces that were already cut to size.

"I'm new in town," Josh commented, knowing he was stating the obvious but hoping to engage Thompson in some friendly conversation. "What do the lads do around here for amusement?"

"Look, *Flynn.*" Thompson gave him a sneer. "I'm here to work. Not to socialize with a Mick." His British accent and bigoted attitude were perfectly clear.

Josh shook his head. So he had to work next to a man who didn't like the Irish. He wondered if Thompson was in the majority around here. He'd have to keep a low profile until he knew for sure.

~

After a dubious beginning, Josh ended up having a good day. The other men didn't seem to have the same bias as Thompson. Josh did occasionally come across the attitude that the Irish were inferior, which surprised him, especially at a railroad. After all, hundreds of Irish had helped lay the rails to join the East and West Coasts of America.

When his shift was over, he walked the couple of blocks back to the boardinghouse. He let himself in the front door and was glad to see Gwen sitting in the parlor by herself. As he entered, she closed the book she was reading and smiled up at him.

"So how was your first day?" she asked.

"Not bad," he replied. "And you?"

"Well…" She scooted to the edge of her seat, her fingers gripping her book. "I have an assignment tomorrow that I'm excited about."

He nodded with interest.

"This young Irish American woman, Kate Barnard, is running for a state office. I've heard the men at the constitutional convention made up the position just for her. No one is actually expected to run against her, but she's coming to Shawnee tomorrow to campaign anyway. My boss wants me to write an article about it."

"That's amazing. A woman is running for a political office?" He leaned against the doorjamb and crossed his arms. "I believe I'll like this new state after all."

Gwen grinned. "I can't wait to hear her speak. She's supposed to be quite an orator."

"It's the Irish in her, you know," he joked.

She chuckled. "I shouldn't be surprised, huh?" She put her book aside. "Would you want to go with me?" She paused, but then hurried on, "I thought you might want to see her."

"I would, at that."

"I've already spoken with Rose. She and Owen are coming too. We'll stop by their store and go with them."

He studied her glowing, pretty face and thought that going anywhere with her would be a pleasure. "It sounds like a grand evening."

~

Gwen retired to her room early. The small foamy-green sanctuary held a creaky black cast-iron bed, a chest of drawers, a small washstand with a mirror, and a colorful braided rag rug. Her accommodations were simple, but she didn't need more.

An idea for a story had been forming in her mind for a few days and she wanted to try her hand at writing it down. She sat at her small desk under the open window, the lace curtain undulating in the breeze. She opened her ink bottle and removed paper from her desk drawer. Her fingers spread across the loose pages to keep them in place. She dipped a pen into the ink and began to write.

She opened the scene with a pirate named Grizzle eyeing a young damsel by the name of Lady Monique van Amsdel. The lady was taking her constitutional by the sea. Gwen had never seen the ocean, but described it with as many flowery adjectives as she could muster. She continued her prose until after Lady Monique had been kidnapped by Grizzle.

Gwen paused and read the scrawled lines out loud. She groaned.

"It's terrible," she muttered to herself.

She crumpled the page and threw it into a wastebasket. The ball of paper joined many other failed attempts. She plopped her arms on her desk and dropped her forehead onto her sleeve.

"Maybe I'm not meant to be a novelist. Everything sounds so silly."

She sighed. She was discouraged. This last inadequate endeavor certainly put a damper on her spirits, but she wasn't ready to give up entirely. She knew she would try again another day.

CHAPTER SEVEN

Gwen and Josh arrived at B & B Mercantile right at closing time. A bell jingled over the door as they entered. It was a typical general store that had everything from boots to tea. It had been opened by and named for Owen's aunt and uncle, Betty and Bob Burke. They had started a second store in Oklahoma City, and Owen was now running the one in Shawnee.

Rose came out of the back room, pushing Hope in a little carriage.

"How is my favorite little person today?" Gwen leaned over the toddler, who babbled back at her.

"Those aren't as good a quality as I'd hoped when I ordered them," Owen said to Josh near the front window.

Gwen turned to see what they were talking about. Josh had a straight-backed chair upside down in his hands and appeared to be studying the workmanship.

"Do you get many requests for furniture?" Josh asked.

"Quite a bit, actually. People usually order it from the catalog."

Josh put the chair down. "If I made some, would you be willing to sell them for me?"

"I don't see why not," Owen replied. "When you get something done, I'll take a look at it. We'll work out the arrangements then."

"I like the sound of that." Josh smiled and shook Owen's hand.

Owen grabbed his suit coat off the counter, ushered everyone out, and locked the door behind them.

"Are we going to walk or ride the trolley?" Gwen asked the group.

"Oh, let's walk. It's such a nice evening and we've been cooped up inside all day," Rose said.

They all agreed. They hurried the several blocks to Woodland Park. On Broadway, they passed the Carnegie Library and the new three-tiered fountain that was over eight feet tall.

A crowd had gathered among the trees. The small group made their way toward the front of the spectators. A podium was placed on a large wooden box for a makeshift platform. Gwen opened her small book and held her pencil at the ready.

Precisely at six thirty, a dapper-looking older gentleman stepped up and introduced the woman the crowd was buzzing about. Kate Barnard was a tiny woman with hair as black as midnight. She was dressed modestly but fashionably in a dove-gray jacket with a flared skirt. Her large hat almost hid her lovely but determined face. Gwen guessed Miss Barnard wasn't more than five years older than herself.

Miss Barnard's voice never wavered as she laid out her plans for the new office. She wanted to make sure children would be protected, that laborers would be treated fairly, and that even prisoners should have humane conditions in which to live. Miss Barnard was decidedly more interesting to listen to than the dry, long-winded politicians of old. As she concluded, hearty applause and cheers of support erupted.

Suddenly a few angry shouts came from the fringe of the group.

"Go home, Irish!" someone hollered.

Josh whirled around with fists clenched.

"Wait, Josh." Gwen grabbed his arm.

Some other men had the two troublemakers by the scruff of the neck.

"Thompson," Josh muttered under his breath.

"Do you know one of them?" Gwen asked.

"I think so, but I'm not positive."

"I can't believe people still talk like that," Gwen fumed.

Miss Barnard was helped down from the stage and escorted to a waiting carriage. The rest of the crowd began to disperse.

Gwen was a little disappointed that she couldn't interview Miss Barnard as she had hoped, but she knew she had taken good notes and still had the makings of a great story.

Gwen glanced down at her little book. "I'd better go on to the office so I can get the story in tonight."

"Of course," Rose agreed. She put a hand on Owen's arm. "We should go home. We'll see you again soon." The little family strolled off to the north on Broadway.

"I'd better go," Gwen told Josh.

"Do you mind some company?" he asked.

"Well...no. I just won't be able to visit while I'm trying to work."

He shrugged. "That's fine with me."

"Let's go then." She smiled and led the way.

$\sim$

When they arrived at the newspaper office, Josh reached out to open the door.

"Mr. Jennings, my editor, should be here. He always stays late," Gwen informed him.

Josh followed her, and a man at a rear desk looked up at them.

"I came in to do that article about Kate Barnard so it can get in tonight's edition."

"Sounds good," her boss replied as he gave Josh a guarded look of interest.

"This is Josh Flynn, an old friend of mine from way back," Gwen explained.

Jennings nodded slowly. "So how is ol' Walter? I haven't seen him in a long time."

"He keeps busy in Guthrie. I can't remember the last time he came down here."

"Hmm. He and I had some good times in Guthrie. I should probably telephone him and see how he's doing."

Gwen sat down at her desk and pulled out some paper, a pen, and ink. "I'm sure he'd like that," she said offhandedly as she flipped open her little notebook.

Gwen went about her business, apparently unaware of the not-so-subtle warning to Josh from Mr. Jennings that Gwen was taken. It almost made Josh want to laugh. But it was a serious matter. Gwen's honor was at stake. He would have to be prudent in everything he did and said.

With her pen, Gwen pointed to a chair nearby. "You can sit over there."

Josh could see that she was already absorbed with her thoughts. Smiling, he sat in the appropriate chair across from her. He picked up an old newspaper, scanned the front page, and then opened it with a snap. Gwen's pen scratched furiously. The only time she paused was when she dipped her pen and tapped it lightly on the ink bottle.

He lowered the newspaper ever so slightly so he could peer over the top. Gwen's brows were furrowed as she wrote. She apparently took her job seriously and put her all into it. She was a bonny lass in many ways.

She looked up suddenly. He thought he had been caught in the act of admiring her, but she didn't seem to notice.

She leaned forward and whispered, "Do you think I should mention the hecklers?"

"No," he said, shaking his head. "I wouldn't waste the ink on those hotheads."

"Mmm…" She nodded and returned to her task.

He lifted the newspaper again to hide his irritation as he remembered those jeering men. He was fairly sure one of them had been Thompson from work. He had recognized the accent. He definitely had an uneasy feeling about him now. If Thompson would try to disturb a political talk, especially one involving a lady, the man couldn't be trusted. Josh decided to keep an eye on him.

Josh heard Gwen rustling around. He dropped the paper for the final time, folded it, and laid it on her desk.

She was reading over what she had written. She must have approved it because she stood and took it to her boss. The editor gave it a glance and a nod of acceptance before putting it in a tray on his desk.

"Good night, Mr. Jennings," she said.

"Good evening, Miss Sanders," he replied. He gave Josh a curt nod before returning to his paperwork.

∼

By the time Gwen and Josh returned to the boardinghouse it was dark. They went around the side yard and paused near the steps of the carriage house.

"Thanks for inviting me tonight. I had a nice time," Josh told her.

"I did too." She smiled.

"It was almost like old times when we used to pal around." There was a hint of nostalgia in his voice.

"It was," she agreed.

He gazed at her, his lips turning up ever so slightly. Gwen could have sworn there was sadness in his eyes. She wondered why.

"I was always curious why you never wrote to me when you left," he said in a guarded manner.

Gwen was startled by his statement. "But I did. Whenever we moved to a new town, I would write and tell you where we were. It was *you* that never wrote back."

He placed his hand over his heart as if he'd been shot. "I never got any letters. Not one."

"I gave them to Mama to mail…" Her chest tightened with the realization that her mother must not have mailed them. All those nights wasted crying into her pillow thinking Josh didn't care for her. She was sickened by the thought.

He appeared as stricken as she felt. "When my parents moved back to Kansas City to help Grandpa Flynn, I was old enough to stay in Guthrie and try to make it on my own, but since I never heard from you I went too. I would have waited…"

"We can't talk about it now," she whispered. "That's in the past."

"But—"

"Gwen!" a voice yelled from the boardinghouse.

Gwen reluctantly turned around. Bevin had the back door open. She stepped out onto the little porch.

"You have a telephone call," Bevin informed her. "It's your man, Walter," she teased.

"Thank you," she told Bevin.

Gwen sighed. She peered up at Josh, who seemed to be trying to collect himself. She headed toward the house while Bevin sashayed her way toward Josh. Gwen glanced back before going in and saw Josh with his hands in his pockets looking down at Bevin.

The screen door slammed behind Gwen as she proceeded to the wooden telephone mounted to the wall near the rear window in the kitchen. She was curious why she would be hearing from Walter so soon after her visit to Guthrie. She picked up the black earpiece.

"Hello?" she spoke loudly into the mouthpiece.

"Good evening, Gwendolyn."

She could barely hear his voice over the static. "How are you? Is something wrong?"

"Why would you ask that?"

"Oh, I don't know. I'm just surprised to be hearing from you."

"Is there something amiss with a man wanting to talk with his fiancée?" He sounded a little put out.

"Of course not, Walter," she said lightly, hoping to appease him.

"That young lady who answered the telephone said you had just returned from some function."

Gwen stared out the window. It was still light enough to see Bevin laughing while Josh appeared to be tolerating her.

"What were you doing tonight?" Walter asked.

"Oh, I just went to a political rally. Kate Barnard gave a speech, and Mr. Jennings wanted me to write an article about it," she remarked as she watched Bevin twirl her finger in a loose tendril of her hair.

"Did you go with anyone?"

"As a matter of fact, I did. Rose and Owen came and—I haven't had the chance to tell you yet. Josh Flynn just moved here. He was a friend when I was a girl. He came also."

"Hmm."

"Now, Walter. There's no need to be like that." She turned from the window, trying to ignore how much flirting Bevin was doing out there. "Josh is perfectly harmless. Besides, we've had this discussion before."

"I know." There was a long lag on his end. "When Tina, Miss Randolph, insinuated there might be someone there, I scoffed at the idea. But now it seems—"

"No. No. No!" Her ire was getting up now. So Tina was the reason for all this. It wasn't until she started working for Walter that his jealousy began. "I told you. He's only an old friend. And he just moved here this weekend." She tried to control her anger. "I won't stand for this. You either trust me or not."

"All right, Gwen," he said in a soothing voice. "There's no reason to get in a dither."

She fumed a moment longer before answering, "Fine."

He cleared his throat. "You said they were going to dedicate your new church. When is that?"

"On May twelfth. Why?"

"I thought I'd come then and visit you."

She felt the fire go out of her. "Really? That would be nice, Walter. You can meet Josh yourself and see how safe I am with him in my midst," she said a tad more sarcastically than she intended.

"I'll plan on it."

"I have to go, Walter. There are things I need to do. I'll talk to you again soon." She tried to sound cheery, but she sure didn't feel that way.

"Good-bye." He almost sounded affronted.

"Good-bye."

She hung the earpiece on the telephone. She heard Bevin give a lilting farewell to Josh. Gwen picked up her skirts and all but ran through the kitchen and up the stairs. For some reason, she just couldn't face anyone. Especially not someone as obviously smitten as Bevin.

CHAPTER EIGHT

As it turned out, May first was during the workweek, so Ada moved her May Day celebration to a Sunday afternoon so everyone could come. That first Sunday in May did not have a particularly outstanding beginning. The sky was cloudless, but the air was damp with humidity.

Owen stopped by the boardinghouse early to tell Gwen that Hope had had a fever in the night so they were going to stay home. He left a pretty white cake that Rose made and his horse and buggy for Josh and Gwen to use for the trek to Luke's.

After church, Gwen fried some chicken in one of Mrs. Brown's cast-iron skillets and cooked some German cabbage. Ada was going to boil some potatoes for mashing and bake bread. Luke was going to make his famous cream gravy. He had practically lived off it while he was a bachelor and had become quite the expert.

Gwen telephoned Luke when the food was ready and told him they were on their way without Rose and Owen. After all the dishes had been packed carefully in Owen's buggy, Josh and Gwen set off. Gwen directed Josh to Kickapoo Street. They drove several miles north, reminiscing the entire time, making the journey seem like a short one.

About halfway to their destination, Gwen spotted some small cup-shaped reddish-purple flowers along the roadside.

"Stop, Josh," she said impulsively. She touched his suit coat sleeve. "I love those flowers. Let's pick some so I can make a chain."

"Sounds fun." He gave her a genuine smile as he stopped the horse.

Gwen's heart filled with happiness as she climbed down and stood in the midst of the colorful display.

Josh came around and chuckled. "'Tis a lovely sight you are."

"Thank you, kind sir." She grinned and dipped into a low curtsy. Her foot tangled in the long, vine-like stalks. She mis-stepped, teetered, and sprawled on her backside into the blossoms. Her first thought was to be mortified, but in a wink she knew there was no reason to be embarrassed around Josh. She laughed at her predicament.

Concern was on Josh's face as he reached down for her hand. "Are you all right?"

"Yes," she said between giggles. "As long as I didn't sit on a bee."

He laughed with her as he hauled her up. He held her by the forearms until she had her footing.

She brushed at her skirts to rid herself of leaves and pollen. She then began pulling the stems. They collected quite a bundle before returning to the carriage.

Sitting with the bounty on her lap, she picked up a short flower and turned to Josh. She leaned over and took his lapel with one hand while putting the stem through the buttonhole with the other. She patted his chest lightly.

"There. 'Tis handsome ye are, Josh Flynn," she said with an attempt at an Irish brogue.

"Many thanks, lass," he returned with a smile.

Gwen couldn't stop herself from beaming up at him. It had been a while since she'd had such a carefree day. "Thanks for coming with me. I think we'll have a memorable day."

He squeezed her hand in an amiable manner. "I believe we will," he stated as he released the brake and they moved forward again.

As they progressed, Gwen made her chain of flowers and draped them around her hat. It wasn't long before they turned off the dirt road to the long, tree-lined lane to Luke and Ada's house. They had a pretty white home nestled in the trees with fields nearby. There was a large barn behind the house and a corral for the horses.

Josh pulled up between the house and the barn. Gwen was just hopping down with Josh's assistance when Luke opened the door on the large rear porch. Luke bounded down the green-painted steps while Ada waved from the doorway.

"Perfect timing," Luke greeted. "The taters are done and ready to mash and the gravy's ready."

"Hello to you too," Gwen teased as she gave him a hug.

Gwen hurried up to Ada as the men greeted each other and gathered the food. She squeezed Ada and placed a hand on Ada's protruding belly.

"How are you?" Gwen asked.

"Good." Ada's eyes sparkled and she whispered, "I've been having pains off and on all week. I think my time is soon."

"How exciting!" Gwen said enthusiastically.

They entered the small kitchen. Ada had the table set with a flawless white damask tablecloth and her good floral-patterned china. A vase of purple bearded irises and wildflowers was placed in the center of the table with two decorative paper-and-lace cornucopias filled with red, white, and yellow flowers lying nearby.

"It's all lovely, Ada."

Ada picked up one of the cornucopias by the blue ribbon handle. "I made these for you and Rose. I hope you'll take one to her."

"Of course. That's so nice of you. They're beautiful. You went to too much trouble for little ole us."

"Nonsense," Ada chided. "You know I like doing creative things like this."

Luke and Josh came through the door with a bang and deposited their treasures next to the wood-burning stove. Ada and Gwen put the meal together and then everyone sat down to enjoy their lunch.

Josh and Luke talked about woodworking while they ate. When the last morsel of cake was eaten, Luke invited Josh out to his barn to take a look at the cradle he was just about finished with and to ask his opinion about something.

"I'd like to see it," Gwen said.

"Let's go." Luke scooted his chair back and helped Ada out of hers. "Do you feel like joinin' us?" he asked his wife.

"Of course." She smiled. She gathered the remains of the leftover bread and said, "I'll take these to my birds while we go."

"Your birds?" Gwen asked with a grin.

"I've become rather attached to the birds around here. I've seen cardinals and meadowlarks, but my favorite is a mockingbird."

"It whistles just like her," Luke added.

"I'll have to hear this," Gwen remarked.

Ada led the way out to the back porch. She stopped at the railing and threw the bread pieces as far out as she could. No birds came right away, but Ada whistled a few high notes and they all heard the song returned from a nearby tree.

"How fun." Gwen laughed. "You'll have to teach it all the musical numbers you know."

Ada's lips turned up. "I just might."

Luke offered his arm to Ada and they walked toward the barn. Near the windmill, Gwen noticed a round red sandstone rock about the size of an apple hanging by a rope from a branch of a cedar tree.

"What in the world is that?" Gwen asked.

"It's my new weather rock," Luke explained proudly as they paused to look at it.

"Your weather rock?" Gwen was curious.

"It tells me the weather," he informed her.

He looked serious, but he surely wasn't. Gwen couldn't help it; she had to ask, "How does a rock tell you the weather?"

"Well…" Luke crossed his arms in readiness to give a scientific explanation. "If it's wet, it means it's rainin'. If it's white, it means it's snowin', and if it's spinnin' around and around, it means there's a tornado."

Josh laughed. Ada smiled but shook her head.

Gwen groaned. "Oh, you! I should have known better."

She whacked him playfully on the shoulder before they went into the dim barn. Luke's horses were in the stalls and whinnied a greeting.

Luke went to a workbench and took a folded sheet off the large cradle. It had solid wood sides. The headboard was taller than the rest and curved. He had also carved a heart in it.

"It's so sweet," Gwen said as she admired it.

"Isn't it?" Ada agreed. "He spent all his spare time for months working on it."

"Well, I'm no carpenter," Luke said as if he needed to make excuses. He glanced at Josh. "I thought I'd put one more coat of varnish on it." He turned the cradle over. "I wanted to see about this blocking. I didn't know if it was braced good enough."

"It should be," Josh said. "But a piece or two across the middle would take care of any worries. It's such a fine size, the baby will be fairly heavy by the time he or she outgrows it."

Luke nodded in agreement. "That's what I thought." He placed it carefully right side up.

Josh walked over to Luke's horses, Samson and Daisy, and patted their noses. Daisy tossed her head and flared her nostrils but before long he had her charmed. Gwen couldn't help but think he must have that influence over every female he met.

In the distance, a train horn blasted its warning at a crossing.

Josh tilted his head and listened. "There are tracks near here?"

"The Santa Fe goes north and south at the back of my prop-erty. It goes north from Shawnee to Aydelotte, Meeker, Payson, and on up to Kansas," Luke said.

Josh nodded. "I didn't think the Rock Island came this way."

They left the barn together. The wind had picked up, and it was cloudier than when Gwen and Josh had made their drive. The cattle in one of Luke's fields had their backsides to the wind.

"Looks like it's about to storm," Luke commented. "I'd better get the Emersons' horse and buggy in the barn."

"We'll go in, and I'll help Ada clean the kitchen." Gwen didn't want to hear talk of storms. Bad weather was not something she liked to think about.

"Sounds good," Luke said as he went to untie the horse's lead rope from the post.

Gwen and Ada proceeded to the house. About halfway up the steps, Ada hesitated. With one hand she grasped the railing and with the other she touched her stomach. There was the slightest grimace on her face before she exhaled and gave Gwen a reassur-ing smile.

"That was a strong one," Ada commented. "I've had a few of those today."

Gwen helped Ada the rest of the way up the steps. She wanted to talk to Ada about what it was like to be with child, but she didn't know if she should ask about something so personal.

"Don't look so worried, Gwen. I'm fine."

"Does it hurt?" Gwen asked in hushed tones.

"It doesn't hurt exactly. It's more like my midsection is tight-ening up."

Gwen opened the door. They went in and began picking up the dishes.

"Are you nervous?" Gwen asked.

Ada's face appeared calm. "I would be lying if I said I wasn't. There are so many things that can happen. But I'm not paralyzed by fear. I'll be able to do it. My body is going to get this baby out. I just need to stay out of the way and let it happen."

There was no end to the admiration that Gwen had for Ada. She knew terrible things could happen during childbirth. Even Owen's first wife had died from complications. Gwen didn't know if she would be so self-assured if she were ever so blessed.

Gwen and Ada had just about completed their task by the time Luke and Josh returned.

"I was beginning to wonder about you two," Ada said as she dried her hands on a dish towel.

Luke held up two barn lanterns. "I thought I'd better trim the wicks and fill these up with kerosene before we came in." He set them on the wooden floor by the table.

"Do you think the storm looks bad enough to go to the dugout?" Ada asked. She placed her hands protectively on her stomach.

"It's hard to tell yet." Luke went to his wife and gave her a hug of reassurance. "Flynn and I are going to the front porch to keep an eye out. We'll have a good view to the southwest from there."

Gwen turned away and began to scrub the last plate. She didn't hear Ada's reply. The dugout? The only reason they would need to go to the dugout that the previous owners had lived in was if a tornado was coming. Homesteaders lived in those tiny damp homes carved into the side of hills out of necessity when they first came to the territory but people only used them now for storage or as shelter from tornadoes.

Gwen's blood ran cold. She was absolutely terrified of tornadoes. She never wanted to relive that horrible, sickening night when, as a little girl, she had witnessed her younger brother, Gordon, and sister, Genevieve, being killed during a tornado. She wished she could erase that night from her memory, but it was forever lurking in the recesses of her mind. The storm had come in the darkness. Her entire family had been in their beds. She awoke to the screaming of her siblings with whom she shared a room. The screeching timbers, the crashing of glass, and the roar of the tornado as it demolished the roof of their house would always be with her.

After the chaos had come total nothingness. She had felt so alone. Pounding rain poured down and her father finally scrambled through the rubble to rescue her from under a huge beam that had stopped just short of landing on her. Her mother's wail still pierced her heart. Her mother had found her brother and sister in the same bed huddled together under splintered wood. Gwen had seen their faces when lightning flashed. She had known they were gone. Her life was forever changed.

It had been too much for them all, especially for her mother. As they were leaving the graveyard, her mother insisted on selling the farm and moving away. Her father had lost his desire to stay, so they sold everything and moved from their home and followed Luke's family to Guthrie.

Gwen had been a bruised, hurt girl when she met Josh. His friendship, cheery ways, and easy demeanor had eventually been the balm she needed. She was finally able to move past the sorrow, but her fear of tornadoes remained.

Ada's voice startled her out of her reverie.

"What was that?" Gwen asked, dazed.

"I said, I think that plate is clean," she said lightheartedly.

"Of course." She gave it to her. "I had something on my mind," she murmured.

"You must have." Ada dried the plate and put it in its place. "I thought I would show you the last few things I've made for the baby, if you like."

"Yes. I would." Gwen put on a brave face. Anything to take her mind off of the weather for a moment was greatly appreciated.

"I'll go get them."

Gwen sighed as Ada walked away. She was glad to have a few moments alone to collect her thoughts.

By the time Ada returned, Gwen was feeling better. They settled onto the sofa, and Gwen fingered one delicate baby gown after another.

"They're just beautiful, Ada," Gwen complimented.

"Thank y—"

Ada was cut off as Luke burst through the front door and commanded, "We have to go. Now!"

CHAPTER NINE

Gwen and Ada were startled by his order, but stood quickly. Ada gathered up all the tiny baby clothes she had spent so many hours hand stitching and put them back in a small cloth bag. She followed Luke toward the kitchen.

"We need to get these lanterns lit," Luke stated.

Gwen's feet wouldn't move. Josh touched her elbow.

"We need to go with them," he said firmly.

She was frightened. She didn't know if she could do it.

He looked into her eyes. "We'll be safe there," he insisted with all certainty.

She nodded. Her mouth was so dry she couldn't speak.

Josh set her in motion. They came up to Luke in time for him to hand them each a lit lantern. The group hurried out the back door. Luke grabbed a shovel and an ax that had been leaning against the porch railing. He carried those items with one hand and assisted Ada with the other.

The wind was ferocious. Gwen felt as if all the pins were being dislodged in her hair. She couldn't worry about modesty as her skirts whirled around her legs because she was so intent on keeping the lantern blocked so it wouldn't snuff out. She did manage to glance over her shoulder. Through the clearing, about a mile away, she could see an enormous black swirling cloud hanging long and low like a curtain blocking the lighter sky beneath. A funnel was taking shape and spinning toward the ground.

Luke got her attention by shouting her name. He nodded toward his weather rock, which was circling madly in the air like agitated wash water. He grinned at her and yelled over the gusts, "I told you it worked!"

Ada gave him a look that said she was not amused. Gwen agreed and gave him a similar glare. He ducked his head and led the way behind the barn to where the land began to rise.

Cut into the small incline was the old dugout. A door seemed to appear out of the earth. The top of the abode was covered with more dirt, weeds, and blooming purple and white irises.

Luke yanked the door open. He took Gwen's lantern and went first down the sandstone steps, swiping cobwebs as he proceeded. He dropped his ax and shovel near the door and held his hand up to Ada. She made her way down and began inspecting the room for vermin in the flickering light.

Gwen followed reluctantly. She was slightly reassured by Josh's supporting hand on her shoulder as she descended into the musty darkness. Josh shut the door behind him. He gave his lantern to Gwen while he helped Luke tie a rope around the door handle and a huge, thick nail that was pounded into a log in the entryway.

Gwen held up the lantern and studied her surroundings. She had seen the outside many times, but had never ventured in because she was not fond of tight spaces. The ceiling was supported by large log timbers. The floor and walls were dug into the rust-colored clay. A long, low bench was on the left side, bins filled with straw and potatoes and onions were along the back, and a shelf with jars of vegetables and fruit lined the right side.

"Our neighbor, Mrs. Engel, is so good to give us her spare canned goods," Ada commented with a smile. "I even helped her can those peaches last year. I'm hoping her culinary talents will rub off on me by association."

Ada's jovial expression was momentarily replaced by one of discomfort.

Gwen went to her side and murmured, "Are you feeling bad?"

"I'm fine. I'm fine," she whispered. "The pains are still far apart. We have enough to worry about right now without being bothered by me."

Luke turned away from the secured door. "Well, we might as well sit and enjoy ourselves."

Luke helped Ada sit on the bench. Gwen sat next to Ada and the men rested on each end. The silence inside stretched as the noise outside increased.

"Me dear old granny used to tell us stories about her trip over from Ireland at times like this. It always helped keep our minds off our troubles when we heard how trying those weeks on a ship were," Josh said.

"What was it like?" Ada asked as she clasped her bag of baby clothes to her chest.

"Something terrible. The quarters were cramped and smelly. They were fairly starved before because of the famine, and things weren't any better on the ship."

Gwen remembered some of his granny's stories. Maybe it would keep her from becoming too frightened if she heard them again. "Tell us about it."

Josh began to regale them with the tales of his grandparents' separate journeys across the sea and the hardships they had endured. They were spellbound by his descriptions.

Gwen wished she could write like that. She could never complete anything because she never felt her attempts were any good. Maybe it was because the content was lacking. If she used real tribulations like the ones Josh's grandparents went through, maybe she would finally have the interesting plot she needed. She had always been fascinated by the subject. She would have to do some research on it.

Her mind was brought to reality all too quickly as the door began to rattle. Luke took his leather work gloves out of his trouser pocket and put them on. He went to the door and grasped the rope in case the knot wouldn't hold.

"Need any help?" Josh asked as he began to rise.

"Not yet."

Josh settled back down.

Driving rain and hail pounded the door. The wind was fierce. Luke strained to keep the door shut. A loud moaning roared in every crevice.

"That sounds like a train," Gwen mumbled.

"That's no train," Josh said quietly.

She didn't realize her hands were cold, clammy, and shaking until Josh's warm, strong hand took hers.

"You'll be fine," he said softly against her ear. "You're not alone."

She shivered. She clutched his hand as if her life depended on it. His confidence radiated through their linked fingers. She began to feel a tiny sense of security and something else she couldn't quite figure out. She had an alarming flash that she was treading on dangerous ground, but she couldn't let go of his hand.

It seemed as if the storm lasted an eternity, but Gwen knew it hadn't been long. Luke was soon able to stop holding the rope. The rain let up.

"It sounds like we can go out now," Luke informed them.

Gwen removed her hand from Josh's. It was still warm from the heat of his. She was suddenly embarrassed by her behavior. She hopped up quickly and brushed her skirts. She avoided looking at Josh by turning her back on him.

"Can we go and see if there's any damage?" Gwen asked Luke.

"I believe that will have to wait," Ada said calmly and quietly.

"Why?" Luke and Gwen asked in unison.

"I think a baby is ready to enter this world."

Luke and Gwen knocked into each other as they bent toward Ada. They helped her up. Josh rushed to untie the rope, and he pushed the door open with his shoulder. As light streamed in, Josh turned down the wicks on the lanterns.

They exited the dark dugout and went into the sprinkling rain. The sky was beginning to clear in the west and sunlight peeked through the sparse clouds. As they walked toward the intact house, they surveyed their surroundings. Limbs had broken and were scattered around. The barn had a hole in the west side near the roof where something had crashed into it. A long piece of lumber was sticking out of one of the trees.

"It looks like we didn't take a direct hit," Luke noted.

"Thank heaven," Ada said gratefully.

As they approached the house, they could see that only a few shingles appeared to be missing.

"Look, darlin'. Your irises." Luke pointed.

Some irises that Ada had planted on the east side of the house were still standing. They were slightly bent and tattered but were still a bright spot amidst the blown leaves and other mess.

"You'll weather your storm, just like they did," he assured her as he put his arm around her.

She nodded and smiled slightly. She stopped walking for a few seconds, seemingly unaware of the concerned faces surrounding her. When she was able, she continued on.

They went into the kitchen. They made Ada sit in a chair while Luke went to the newly installed telephone in the hallway. Gwen paced while wringing her hands. Josh tried to stay in the background.

"Hello? Hello?" Luke all but shouted into the telephone. He turned to Josh and handed the earpiece to him. "Do you know anything about these things?"

Josh listened for a moment. "It's dead. A line must have blown down in the storm."

"The only reason I got one of those blamed contraptions was for this reason." He nodded toward his wife. "I'll go for the doctor, Ada."

"I'll do it," Josh offered.

"No. Both of you stay put," Ada said authoritatively.

"Now, darlin'," Luke began.

"No, Luke. If there was a tornado between here and Shawnee, someone might need a doctor more desperately than we do."

"Ada." It was apparent Luke didn't agree with her.

"Women have been doing this since the beginning of time. I can do it. Especially if I have you and Gwen here."

"Thanks for the vote of confidence," Gwen muttered. She was *not* ready to help someone birth a baby.

Josh stepped forward and squatted down in front of Ada. He placed a hand on hers. "How about if I go and see if I can even find the doctor? If he's too busy, I'll not bring him back."

Another contraction must have hit her because her eyes had a far-off look for a moment before she nodded. "Thank you," she said gratefully.

"I'll saddle my horse," Luke said.

Josh stood, and he and Luke shot out of the house like a cannonball.

"Oh, Ada, I hope the doctor comes. I don't know anything about this. I know I was raised on a farm, but my mother would never let me see anything of that nature. She wouldn't even let me see our cat have kittens," Gwen babbled.

Ada chuckled. "Don't worry." She pushed herself up from her chair. "The last time I saw Dr. Maxwell, I had a whole long list of questions for him in case something like this should occur."

"I still don't know."

"Come." Ada took her arm. "Let's go get the bedroom ready, and I'll tell you everything I know."

CHAPTER TEN

Josh reined Luke's horse Samson, a strong and well-trained gelding, toward the south. Debris was scattered everywhere. There was a dead cow in the ditch. He hoped it didn't belong to Luke.

As he rode on, he came to a tree that had been uprooted and fallen across the road. Wagons wouldn't be able to drive through. Maybe he should move it so the road would be passable. Someone might have a life-or-death emergency and wouldn't be able to make it. He dismounted, loosened the rope from the saddle, and walked to the tree. He tied one end of the rope to a thick branch and the other around the saddle horn before he climbed back up. He clucked his tongue and maneuvered the horse in the right direction.

"Come on, boy. Let's see if we can get this thing out of the way."

It took a couple of attempts before the large horse stepped forward and strained against the rope. The tree wavered and finally gave way so they could pull it to the side.

"Good boy." Josh patted Samson's neck.

He dropped to the ground. He wondered how many times he might have to do this before he arrived in town. As he untied the rope, his mind went back to the reason for his mission. He hoped

Ada would be safe, especially since he had no idea where to begin looking for the doctor. His thoughts turned to Gwen. The terror in her eyes during the storm had been agonizing to watch and he hoped he had been some comfort to her. He hurried his movements. He wanted to get back as soon as possible, but he had the feeling it would be a long while before he returned.

~

"It's a girl!" Gwen shouted with excitement as the tiny, slippery newborn slid onto the pristine towel in her hands.

She wiped the baby's face with an edge of the towel. The little one made a gurgling sound but did not cry. Gwen's heart dropped. "She's not breathing. She's not breathing!" she exclaimed in alarm.

"Luke!" Ada said fearfully from the bed.

Luke, who had been standing by Ada's side, rushed to Gwen's aid. He grasped the baby gently but firmly. He wiped slime from the baby's mouth with his little finger. He turned her over and patted her back. The newborn sputtered, coughed, and finally let out an indignant howl.

"Oh…" Gwen sighed. Her legs wouldn't hold her any longer. She sank into the nearby rocking chair. "How did you know what to do?" Gwen asked.

"It's not all that different than helpin' a calf into the world." He glanced up at his wife's tired face and winked. "Not *much* different."

Luke was surprisingly adept at cleaning the baby. He was extremely precise as he tied and cut the cord. He then lovingly wrapped his daughter in a clean towel.

"Now you're snug and warm, aren't you, my little darlin'?" Luke spoke softly to her as he held her close.

He took her to Ada and laid the infant gently in her arms. "What are you goin' to name her?" Luke asked as he eased himself onto the bed next to Ada.

Ada kissed the baby's head and looked thoughtfully at Luke. "I'd like to name her after you."

He grinned. "Lucas isn't a very pretty name for a gal."

Ada smiled slyly. "I was thinking more along the lines of Lucinda."

"Lucinda? Lucy...Lucy Logan. I like it. How about a middle name?"

"Do you have anything in mind?" Ada asked.

"Iris," he declared with assurance.

"Iris? For my flowers?"

"Well...partly. It did my heart good to see you tend to those plants like I know you'll mind the little one." He kissed them both tenderly. "But another reason is because of your eyes. They're what pulled at my heartstrings in the first place."

"Oh, Luke," Ada whispered as a tear rolled down her cheek.

Gwen snuck out as quietly as she could. She didn't want to intrude any longer. She went into the kitchen. She took off the bloodstained apron she had been wearing and put it in a pan to rinse out before the stains set in.

She felt such a rush of emotions. She was happy for Luke and Ada and relieved the delivery was over. But the overwhelming feelings that overcame her were sadness and jealousy.

It took her a minute as she sorted out why. It was Walter. He just wasn't a demonstrative type of man like Luke. She longed for Walter to look at her that way and say those types of things to her. Maybe if she talked to him about it or was more affectionate or flirtatious toward him, he would respond.

Until she had seen her friends fall in love, she had assumed that this rush of emotion would come after she married. It had been perfectly clear as she watched Ada and Luke and Rose and Owen that her friends actually felt the love and attraction they displayed for one another, even if it was only by the merest glance. She was so ready to feel that way.

The parlor clock chimed nine times. She was amazed. She had assumed it was much later.

She put some wood in the stove and filled the coffeepot with water and put it on to boil. She found the coffee beans and put a scoop into the grinder, then turned the crank on top until it was finished.

Taking a knife out of a crock filled with utensils, she began to slice some bread. She knew Luke would be famished by now and she would put some kind of meal together.

There was a loud rap at the back door. Gwen went to open it and found Josh and Dr. Maxwell standing there.

"Good evening, Dr. Maxwell. How are things in town?" Gwen asked as she let them in.

"Not as bad as I anticipated. The tornado touched down on mostly open land between here and Shawnee. The Asts lost a barn, and I helped a few folks with minor injuries," the physician said. Removing his hat, he placed it on the table before he brushed his thinning gray hair in place.

"That's a relief," Gwen commented.

"Yes. Now, how is our mother?"

"She had a baby girl a few minutes ago."

"I'll see to them both," Dr. Maxwell said.

"Yes. Of course." She led him to the bedroom and shut the door behind him.

Gwen walked back down the short hallway. Josh was sitting at the table. He looked as weary as she felt. She sat down across from him.

"You made it, I see," Gwen commented.

"I did at that. There were trees and other things in the road. It took a long time to get there. I don't believe we should try to make it back in the buggy in the dark. The doctor rode his horse and we still had a hard time of it."

Gwen nodded. "That's fine with me. But Rose will be worried."

"I thought of that, so I stopped by their house to tell them while I was searching for the doctor."

"Good," she said. She sighed and began to rise. "I'll fix us something to eat."

Josh placed his hand on her arm and restrained her. "It can wait. You look all done in."

"Gee, thanks." She sat down again. She patted her hastily repaired hair. "I must look a fright."

"That's not what I meant." His eyes expressed only compassion and worry. "Was the tornado too much to bear?"

Her first reaction was to display indifference, but when she saw his genuine concern, her shoulders slumped. She absentmindedly smoothed the tablecloth. "It was difficult...I could see that night...my brother and sister...the grief of my parents...all of it... as if it had only just happened." She shuddered. "It was terrible."

He placed his hands gently over hers. "I wish I could take the pain for you," he said sincerely.

Gwen was touched that he would say such a thing. She couldn't ask for a better friend. She gave him a tired smile.

The bedroom door opened. Gwen jerked her hands back as if she had touched fire. Luke appeared in the hallway with a small bundle in his arms. Gwen jumped up. She hoped Luke hadn't seen them in such a cozy way. She knew it would appear more inappropriate than it actually was.

Luke came up to them. "The doc's with Ada now. He said little Lucy is the picture of health."

"Oh good," Gwen said as she took another peek at Lucy, who was sleeping.

"Come and see my little gal, Flynn," Luke said proudly.

Josh joined them and peered at the red-faced newborn. "She is lovely at that. There's not a fairer maiden in the territory, I'll grant you." Josh smiled.

Luke was pleased. "That's what I thought." He looked Josh in the eye. "I'm mighty thankful you went for the doc. I'll never forget your help today."

"'Twas nothin'. I was glad to do it."

Dr. Maxwell came out of the bedroom and walked up to them. "Mrs. Logan has lost a goodly amount of blood. She will be weak. She should not push herself for several days. She should have some help if you can get it," he informed Luke.

"I can stay," Gwen piped up.

The doctor nodded. "I will come out sometime tomorrow to see how she is progressing."

"Thank you. I'll walk you out, Doc. I've got to get the chores done." Luke handed Lucy to Gwen.

"It's late. I'll help," Josh offered.

The three men went out the rear door. Gwen took Lucy into the parlor. She sat in the upholstered golden-oak rocker. Lucy stirred and gave a grunt of annoyance. The baby opened one eye for a moment before closing it and settling into Gwen's arms.

Gwen smiled. She had never been one to gush over babies, unlike other females she knew. She had been old enough when her twin brothers were born to realize the hard work involved in raising children. But her heart warmed through and through as she held the warm baby.

Newborns were not especially pretty creatures. Nevertheless, Gwen could see the definite potential in Lucy. The baby had oval eyes, a delicate nose, pretty little lips, and tiny ears. The small amount of hair on her head was light and fair, maybe even with a reddish tint to it.

She felt a surge of protectiveness and yearning course through her veins for the innocent, defenseless infant. She could see now what a blessing these little people were. Maybe she was ready to be a mother after all. She wondered for a split second what kind of father Walter would be. She couldn't quite picture it in her mind's eye, so she put that notion aside and touched Lucy's cheek.

"Welcome, little Lucy," Gwen said softly. "You will be *so* loved."

~

Josh quietly let himself into the kitchen. Luke had asked him to tell Gwen about Ada. Gwen wasn't in the kitchen. He crept down the hallway, not wanting to disturb Ada or the baby.

He found Gwen sitting in the front room rocking Lucy and humming to her. Gwen's hair was slightly untidy and her clothes were rumpled a bit, but the serene expression on her face made her a vision to behold. She was lovelier than he had ever let himself imagine over the years.

He doubted she even knew just how beautiful she was. He could hear her laugh it off if he were ever to say anything of the sort. He wished he could tell her, but he would never be able to do that. She was taken. Her heart belonged to another man. Exhaling, he tried to expel his frustration.

He must have made a loud enough noise for her to hear, because Gwen looked up. She didn't appear to notice that he had been staring at her. He was glad of that.

He cleared his throat and said, "Luke wanted you to check on Ada soon."

"Yes, I will," she agreed.

"I'd better get back out there," he said, feeling awkward all of a sudden.

She nodded and gazed back at the baby.

He turned and marched away, knowing that Gwen was oblivious to any warm thoughts he was having about her.

CHAPTER ELEVEN

Josh left early the following morning, taking Owen's buggy with him. Since the telephone was still inoperable, Gwen had asked him to tell Mr. Jennings she wouldn't be in for a few days. Gwen cooked and cleaned for Ada and tried to assist in any way she could. It wasn't until midweek that they heard from anyone in the outside world. They had all been sitting on the front porch enjoying the sunshine and the gentle breeze when the telephone shattered the silence.

Luke jumped up and ran in to answer it, only to return moments later.

"It's for you, Gwen," he stated as he sank into his chair.

"For me?" Gwen asked, wondering if Rose or Josh were checking on things.

"It's Manning."

"Oh." She almost blushed as she hurried down the hallway. She was surprised Walter would take the time to telephone her in the middle of the day. She smoothed her hair and almost laughed at her foolishness. It wasn't as if he could see her.

"Hello?" Gwen spoke into the telephone as she held the other part to her ear.

"Gwendolyn?" Walter asked.

"Yes, Walter. How are you?"

"I'm fine, of course," he replied. "I heard there was a tornado near Shawnee."

"Yes. As far as I know there wasn't much damage. The telephone line has been down out here, though."

"I know. I've been trying to reach you since Monday."

She was touched that he had done that. "I'm glad you finally got through."

"I am also. When Jennings called me to say you weren't able to come to work, I wondered what had transpired. Someone at your boardinghouse said you were staying at the Logans'." There was almost an accusatory tone in his voice. She decided to ignore it.

"Yes. Ada and Luke are the parents of a beautiful baby girl, Lucy. I've been helping out."

"That is altruistic of you."

She couldn't tell if he was teasing or not. "You know how much Luke and Ada mean to me. It's been no trouble at all." She almost felt as if she were defending herself for some reason.

"Are you going to return to Shawnee by Saturday morning? I'll be on the eleven o'clock train."

"Yes. Yes," she said quickly to cover up the fact that she had forgotten he was coming so soon. "I'll be there."

"Good."

"I'm glad you're coming, Walter," she said sincerely.

"It's time I came to see you."

"Yes. It is," she agreed.

"Until Saturday then?"

"I'll see you then. Good-bye." She placed the earpiece on the hook.

Crossing her arms, she leaned her back against the wall. It had been a strange conversation. It almost felt as if he were only verifying her whereabouts instead of wanting to be reassured of his loved one's safety. She didn't want to make more out of his words than was evident, though, so she would just look forward to his rare visit. She also wanted to try her hand at being more carefree around him, in hopes he would return the sentiment. She grinned at the prospect. It would be fun to flirt with her fiancé. She couldn't wait.

~

Saturday was an agreeable day for early May. The temperature was pleasant. Abundant fluffy white clouds moved lazily across the endless blue sky.

Gwen was actually early as she awaited Walter's train. She'd had a busy morning already. She had rented a surrey at Mr. Carey's livery, put together a picnic lunch, and changed into a new plum-colored suit and white shirtwaist. She was ready for a relaxing day with Walter.

She watched from the platform of the station as the engine came into view and stopped in a fog of steam and smoke. Finally she spotted Walter's tall, wide-shouldered physique and rushed to greet him. She flung herself into his arms. He had to take a step or two backward to keep them from falling.

"Gwen!" His voice was surprised.

She impulsively kissed his cheek, knocking both of their hats askew.

"My, my," he commented with a small smile as he placed her aside and put her hand properly in the crook of his arm. "What warrants such a warm greeting? In public, no less?"

"I'm just glad you're here. I missed you." She grinned.

"I share the same sentiments, my dear."

"I have a fun day planned. I thought we'd take a ride in the country and have a picnic." She looked up at him with anticipation.

He nodded. "First let me have my trunk delivered to the Norwood Hotel."

"Yes, of course," she agreed.

After the arrangements were made with the coach driver from the Norwood, Gwen and Walter drove north on Broadway. She sat closely next to him as he drove the surrey. They passed Woodland Park. When they went by Owen and Rose's house, she pointed it out to him. They kept driving as the homes became fewer and farther between.

When they had gone about a mile, Gwen motioned to her favorite house in town on the east side of the road. It was a Queen Anne–style house with wraparound porches on both stories. A large round tower ascended skyward at the front of the house. Patterned wood shingles and wooden clapboards encased the building.

"I just love that house." She sighed as she admired it.

"It's nice. I prefer the clean lines of more modern accommodations myself."

"Oh," she said quietly. She was a tad disappointed that he didn't share her admiration of such fine architecture.

She gave it one last glance before she said, "I thought we'd picnic over there." She waved her hand at a lone tree in a meadow sprinkled with white and yellow wildflowers.

He pulled to a stop and set the brake in the sparse shade under the tree. He glanced down at his gray suit. "I'm not attired for a country ramble. Could we dine in the buggy?"

"Of course," she said brightly. She pushed the blanket off the top of the basket at her feet. She dug through it and handed him a ham sandwich wrapped in white paper.

As they ate their meal, Gwen asked about his family in Tennessee. He told her the last he had heard, his parents were fine except for his father's arthritis still plaguing his shoulder. He asked about her family, saying he had seen her brothers buying peppermint sticks at the store recently.

She chuckled. "Mother indulges them more than she ever did me."

He smiled. "Speaking of indulgences..." he began mysteriously, "I have just about decided to buy a horseless carriage."

"Really?" She had to admit she thought the purchase was rather extravagant. "I thought we were saving for a house."

"We'll have enough," he assured her. "Miss Randolph knows of a fellow in Oklahoma City who needs some ready cash and wants to sell his."

"Hmm…Well, if you think it's prudent."

"Why wouldn't it be? There will be no animals to feed and keep healthy and no stalls to muck. It seems an intelligent decision to me."

Gwen nodded even though she didn't entirely agree. Thinking that Tina Randolph had something to do with his unexpected desire for an automobile didn't endear Gwen to the idea. The thought of Tina did spur her on, though, reaffirming the need to be more affectionate.

Removing her hat, she bided her time. She waited until Walter had taken his last sip of apple cider. She returned his empty mug to the basket.

"We should make our way back to town, don't you agree?" He began to reach for the reins.

"What's the hurry?" Gwen asked lightly as she grabbed his hands and held them tightly. "I…I thought it would be nice to… to…" She couldn't bring herself to say the words. Instead, she leaned toward him and kissed him quickly on the lips.

She opened her eyes, half expecting to see disapproval in his gray ones. Instead she was encouraged by the look he gave her. She inched closer. He reached for her, held her face in his hands, and smiled slightly before he placed his lips securely on hers. They tarried over each other for a moment before Walter backed away.

He peered over his shoulder. "I think I hear someone. We'd better go before I ruin your reputation," he jested.

"Yes, Walter." She grinned as she retrieved her hat. "I'm so glad you came for a visit."

He squeezed her hand before setting the horse in motion. "I agree."

CHAPTER TWELVE

Josh thought he was arriving early enough for the dedication of St. Benedict Church, but as he joined the throng he could see there were no more seats available in the pews. He made his way up the stairs and found a place in the gallery near the choir. He waved at Rose when he spotted her with the other choir members.

He settled into his seat and admired the workmanship of the building. The white walls led to a multi-arched ceiling. Sunlight filtered through blue and pale-amber glass windows high above the white altar at the west end. The pews were polished to a shine and crammed with people in their finest frocks of every hue. It was quite a colorful scene.

By the time the service began, people were standing in the aisles and in the stairway. There had to be more than a thousand people in attendance. Josh didn't know if he would ever find Gwen in such a crowd, but he finally caught sight of her near the front in her familiar hat and golden-colored suit. The man next to her must be her fellow. He couldn't really see him from his vantage point, but Josh was of the opinion that her man was a little too barrel-chested for his suit coat, as it strained across his shoulders.

He wondered when he would be introduced to her intended. She had kept him to herself yesterday and didn't bring him by the boardinghouse. She had left early this morning to fetch him. He wanted to meet the man. It suddenly occurred to him that he needed to evaluate Mr. Manning. If he didn't approve of Gwen's choice, he would tell her, whether she liked it or not.

The orchestra from Sacred Heart Abbey began the first strains of music along with the organ. The sound was grand. He decided he'd better stop thinking of Gwen for the moment and enjoy the event.

Afterward, Josh filed slowly out along with the rest of the crowd. He scanned the mass of people for Gwen, but couldn't see her. He headed for the refreshment tables that were set up under long canvas tents on the grounds. After waiting patiently in line, he at last found Gwen serving punch.

"Good morning, Josh," she greeted him gaily. "Isn't this mad? Have you ever seen so many people?" She gave him a glass and nodded toward the church. "Luke and Walter are over there."

The two men were standing in a thin line of shade on the north side of the building. He sauntered over to them. Luke was holding Lucy, who was sleeping peacefully in her proud father's arms.

"Mornin', Flynn," Luke said in his easy way. "Have you met Gwen's fiancé yet? This is Walter Manning."

Josh shifted his cup to his left hand and extended his right. Manning had a strong grip. "I'm Josh Flynn."

"He's an old friend of Gwen's," Luke added.

"I've heard," Manning stated with what seemed like a forced smile. "You work for the railroads?"

Josh gave him a friendly grin. "I work in the cabinet shops."

"Hmm."

Silence began to stretch between the men.

"Speakin' of carpentry work…" Luke began, "I had this huge old red oak tree on the place that died a few years back. The storm finally blew it over. Do you believe you'd like it for anythin'?"

"As a matter of fact, I would. I'd like to make some furniture and try to sell it in Emerson's store," Josh said.

"Sounds like a good idea. What are you goin' to try your hand at?"

"I thought maybe a table and some chairs," Josh said.

"That's pretty darn ambitious. I couldn't do it," Luke commented.

"I'll make a piece at a time. Owen wouldn't have room for the entire set anyway," Josh explained.

"That's right. What style are you thinkin'?" Luke asked.

"I haven't decided yet. Something fairly simple with turned legs, and I might carve a design on the chair backs."

"Sounds right nice." Luke nodded. "I'll cut the tree in long lengths and bring a load by the next time I come to town."

Manning, who had observed them but hadn't joined the conversation, took a fancy gold pocket watch out of his vest. After noting the time, he snapped it shut.

"Gentlemen, it's time I take my leave. I can't miss the train. I have to be in court in the morning," Manning stated with importance. He tipped his hat before striding over to Gwen to say his farewells.

Gwen gave Manning an affectionate grin and brushed something from his coat sleeve. She whispered something in his ear before he departed. She waved at him as he disappeared into the crowd.

"Friendly fella, ain't he?" Luke commented wryly.

"I assumed it was my company he didn't care for."

"Nah. He's just that way. Always has been," Luke informed him.

"What does she see in him?" It was a moment before Josh realized he had asked the question out loud.

Luke shrugged. "I don't know. I always wondered that myself." He shifted Lucy in his arms. "From what I gather, Aunt Grace was the one who 'encouraged' them to court."

"You don't say…" Josh mumbled.

"They've been engaged for a couple of years. For the life of me, I don't know what the holdup has been. You'd think a man who has found the love of his life wouldn't want to wait," Luke reflected.

"I agree."

Josh drained his drink. His eyes followed Gwen as she traded places with another lady and put on an apron before going to the table set up to wash the dishes.

"I'd better take my glass back. They'll be needing it," Josh said.

"I was just thinkin' I ought to find Ada over at the pastry table and make sure she's not overdoin' it."

They walked off together and parted company as they neared Gwen.

"I thought you might need this." Josh gave her the cup.

"Yes. Thank you." As she took it from him, her wet fingers dripped water on his. After cleaning the cup and setting it upside down on a nearby towel to dry, she wiped her hands on her apron and turned to him with a gleam in her eyes.

"So you met Walter?" she asked expectantly, almost as if she wanted his opinion. A favorable one, that is.

"Aye. A quiet man he is," Josh said carefully.

She appeared surprised by the observation, but must have quickly thought it over because she said, "I guess you're right. He's not one for frivolous conversation."

"I'm always one for a good laugh or tall tale myself," he said, waiting to see what her reaction would be.

"I am at times, but I've realized I need to be the dignified woman my mother raised me to be," she said in her nonchalant manner.

Josh was unexpectedly saddened by that simple statement. He hated to think Gwen would change her carefree demeanor to please others. He wanted to tell her she shouldn't do that to herself, but he knew it wasn't the time or the place. He'd bite his tongue for now.

Rose came up to them with a tray full of dirty dishes and handed them to Gwen.

"How are you today, Josh?" Rose asked.

"I'm glorious, after hearing you sing as fair as the angels this morning," he complimented.

With a slight flush to her cheeks, she smiled and said humbly, "Thank you. I loved having the small orchestra with us. Wasn't the music lovely?"

"Yes. It was grand," he agreed.

Another woman came toward them with more dirty dishes.

"I'd better get out of the way," Josh said. "Is Owen about?"

"Yes. He's around here somewhere with Hope." Rose looked but didn't see her husband.

"I'll take a stroll and see if I can come across him. Good day, ladies." He tipped his hat to them.

He did as he proposed, but didn't find Emerson as he ambled around the small acreage surrounding the church. Instead, he spotted Bevin sitting on a quilt under a tree. She was a lovely vision, to be sure. Her pale-violet cotton frock was simpler than those of the other ladies, and she was lazily fanning herself with her straw hat. She waved furiously when she saw him.

"Mornin' to ye, Josh. Would you care to join me for a bite of scone?" Bevin asked with a broad smile as she opened a picnic basket.

"You're not expecting anyone else to share your bounty?" He eyed the plate of scones that she uncovered.

"Well...no...that is...I wondered if you might stop by," she said demurely.

She cut the scone and placed a wedge on a blue-checkered napkin.

"Sorry, I've no clotted cream or butter. I was afraid it'd spoil in the heat, but I do have strawberry jam." She opened the jar and put a spoon inside.

He put on a liberal dollop of jam and took a big bite. The dry, crumbly scone didn't compare with Gwen's, but he smiled at Bevin's efforts. He finished it to stave off his hunger, but politely refused another piece. He gladly accepted a mug of tepid lemonade.

"So what brings you here to this fair city?" he asked before he sipped the tart drink.

"That's a long tale, it is." She pinched off a tiny piece of the scone and nibbled it.

"I've the time, if you've the breath," he encouraged as he lounged back against the tree and crossed one boot over the other.

"Well...the short of it is that I had a beau, Patrick, for three years, and I finally told him I was of the mind to marry and keep house for him instead of for me widowed da, and he said he wasn't ready to tie himself down. After *three* years, mind you!" Fire flashed in her blue eyes. "What kind of man does that, I ask you?" She didn't wait for an answer before continuing. "I told me da that me younger sisters were old enough to take over the chores and that I didn't want to see that eejit again. Me da has a cousin that works at the Norwood Hotel and she secured me a position in the restaurant there. So I moved here happily from Oklahoma City."

Josh nodded slowly and tried to show the appropriate amount of sympathy. He took a drink to hide a smile. He couldn't shake the feeling that her old fellow had probably gotten the tongue-lashing of his life after that fiasco.

"So, here I am." She paused dramatically. "I'm jilted by me love...makin' me own way in life." She sighed loudly.

Josh tried so hard not to laugh he choked on his lemonade. He leaned forward, covering his mouth, and she pounded him on the back.

"I—" He gasped and coughed some more. "I'm fine," he whispered hoarsely, hoping she hadn't dislocated his shoulder. She was mighty for one so tiny. "It's an admirable thing for a woman to have a respectable job."

"Well, it'll do for now, but I don't *intend* to be an old maid," she said vehemently. She suddenly ducked her head, seemingly ashamed of her outburst. She glanced at him sheepishly. "That is…I pray the saints and the angels will guide me true love straight into me waitin' arms."

His lips turned up. "Indeed. I'm sure they will." Heaven help them if they didn't.

She reached over and grasped his arm. "I was wondering if you—"

"Hello, you two!" Gwen interrupted from afar. She made her way up to them and nodded toward her empty tray. "I'm going around collecting dishes."

"We have our own here," Bevin said curtly.

Gwen noticed Bevin's fingers clutching Josh's arm. Her smile faltered for a moment. "I'll let you be then. There's so much to do." She swiveled with a swirl of skirts and took off at a quick pace.

Josh brushed Bevin off his arm more forcefully than he'd intended. She all but fell over.

"Wait, Gwen!" He scrambled to his feet and chased after her.

"Josh Flynn!" Bevin bellowed from behind him.

Josh caught up with Gwen in a few strides. He touched her shoulder and said, "Gwen, wait. It's not what it appears."

She stopped to face him. Her head was held high, but the gleeful demeanor that he had seen previously was missing. "Honestly, Josh," she began, "it doesn't matter. You're unattached and she is too." She moved away. "I have work to do. Go. Have fun with your lady friend."

Gwen disappeared into the crowd as no words came to him to stop her. He glanced up at the sky and shook his head before striking off for home.

CHAPTER THIRTEEN

Life was back to normal for Gwen for the next couple of weeks. The only exception was the telephone calls from Walter every couple of days. He had never done that before. He didn't have much to say, except that he wanted to see how she was doing.

One afternoon toward the end of the month, Gwen found herself standing in the middle of Bell Street between Main and Ninth on an assignment for the newspaper. The Oklahoma State Humane Society had donated a gray granite humane water fountain for horses and other animals. She took notes about the height and estimated the basin was about six feet wide. Water flowed from the mouths of four bronze lion heads. Horses could drink without being unharnessed, and at the base there was a small depression where dogs and other animals could quench their thirst.

She smiled and shook her head as she closed her notebook and put it and her pencil in her skirt pocket. It was an inconsequential assignment about a silly fountain, but she would write the best article she could because it wouldn't be right to do otherwise. She walked toward Ninth Street and turned left.

She heard the clanging of a bell and saw the fire department's pump wagon rush out of the station. Horses' hooves clattered as they galloped west. She hurried to the corner and watched them go.

She asked a bystander, "Do you know where they're going?"

"Heard there was a fire at the Rock Island yards," the older woman said.

Her heart skipped a beat.

Picking up her skirts, she sprinted. It was not ladylike, she knew, but she had to make sure Josh wasn't in harm's way. She made it less than a block before she had to pause and catch her breath. If her corset wasn't so tight she would be able to run as fast as she did when she was a girl. She continued on as fast as she could, trying to ignore the stitch in her side.

She followed the billowing smoke and the commotion of men. She tripped over the tracks—graceful as usual—and luckily righted herself before falling on her face. The intense fire was southeast of the pond in the yards. The firemen were using their hoses while the railroad men were using buckets to combat the blaze.

"What happened?" Gwen asked a light-haired young man who was watching.

"Aw, some chaps in the store department piled up some boxes and barrels to burn, but it got out of hand," he said with a British accent. "They were afraid the oil house over there would catch fire." The young man shook his head in disgust and stuck his hands in his pockets before he realized he was talking to a person of the fairer sex. He straightened to his full height of about five feet six inches and stroked his peach fuzz of a mustache. "I'm Chuck Thompson, miss. What brings a pretty lady like you out here?" he asked.

"I am a reporter for the *Globe*." She quickly retrieved her notebook and pencil. "I'd better go investigate further," she said in her most professional manner as she tried to lose herself in the crowd. Gwen had always been leery of men who were overly friendly.

She found a good vantage point on top of a pile of gravel. The railroad men had a bucket line from the pond. Water sloshed as pails were passed from hand to hand. It was then she saw Josh, right in the midst of the line. He was working intently as he passed buckets and she could tell even from a distance that he was soaking wet.

Josh and the other men worked for quite a while until the fire was extinguished. She wanted to talk to Josh before she went back to the office, so she tried to descend the little mountain, but gravel dislodged and she began to slide.

A hand reached up and caught her flailing arm. "Careful, there, miss," the man named Thompson said as he helped her down the rest of the way.

"I…uh…thank you," Gwen stuttered as she removed her arm from his grip. She returned her notebook and pencil to her pocket, and she brushed at her skirts.

"It was quite a spectacle, was it not?" he asked.

"Yes. Everyone was brave."

"Well, now, I don't know about that. It wasn't a large fire."

"I thought it was. If any of those embers had floated over to the oil house, it would have been disastrous." She shuddered to think about the consequences.

"Thompson," Josh's familiar voice interrupted from behind her.

"Flynn," Thompson uttered without any warmth.

"If you'll excuse us," Josh said before placing a hand on Gwen's back.

"The young miss and I are having a conversation." Thompson pursed his lips in disapproval.

"Yes, but I should be getting back," Gwen informed him.

"I'll see you safely on your way, Gwen." He pressed her forward.

She was surprised by Josh's abruptness with a fellow employee, but she was also glad to escape. They walked as quickly as they could over the terrain.

"What brings you out here?" Josh asked as he glanced over his shoulder.

"The fire, of course." She smiled. "I had to see if…everything was fine."

"Aye," he paused, giving her a weary grin. "The fire department was the saving factor. We couldn't have done it without them."

Mud had splattered on his trousers, shirt, and face. She wished she had a hankie with her. Instead, she reached up and wiped the mud off his chin with her thumb.

"You're wet," she stated in a motherly way.

"I'll dry." He smiled.

"You'll catch your death of cold," she admonished.

He chuckled. "It's hot as Hades today. I believe I'll survive."

"You might at that." She waggled a finger in front of his nose. "But you come straight home after work and get some dry clothes on."

"Yes, ma'am." He hung his head and took on the part of a penitent schoolboy.

She laughed. "I'd better go. I have a couple of stories to write."

"I'm glad you came by to check on…things," he said.

She nodded. "I'm relieved you're safe." She waved as she began her trek to the newspaper office.

Josh turned around to go back to the shop. He was just about to go in the door when Thompson suddenly appeared in front of him, blocking the way.

"So was that lady a friend of yours?" Thompson asked, puffing up his chest.

"Aye." Josh didn't feel he needed to explain his history with Gwen.

"Is she *only* a friend? Is she spoken for?" Thompson sneered. "I'd fancy a lady friend myself."

"She's taken." Josh stepped forward and glared down at the wee blackguard. "You'll not be trying to find her."

"I already know where to find her. I know what her name is and where she works," he said complacently.

"You'll not be bothering the lady," Josh said curtly. He was beginning to tire of Thompson's arrogant demeanor.

"We'll see." Thompson cocked an eyebrow.

Josh clenched his fists at his sides. "I said, you will leave her alone," he ground out.

"And who will stop me?" Thompson goaded.

Josh took a step forward and stared down at Thompson's smug, upturned face. He spoke through gritted teeth, "I will. You worthless—"

"All right, men." Mr. Miller clamped a hand on Josh's shoulder. "Cool off, you two. Go on up, Thompson. I'll talk to you in a minute. Flynn, come with me."

Josh instantly regretted letting Thompson get his ire up. He followed his boss around the corner of the building, where they stopped.

Mr. Miller crossed his arms and took an authoritative stance. "Now, Flynn, I know you're a hard worker and I also know Thompson is the instigating type, but I won't have any fighting in my shop. If so, one of you will have to go, and since you're the new man…"

Josh nodded contritely. "Yes, sir. I understand."

"I knew you would," Mr. Miller said approvingly. "Let's see if we can get some work done before the day is over."

"Yes, sir." Josh grinned, relieved that his reprimand was over. "I should be able to finish that bench today."

Mr. Miller smiled. "Well, get after it then."

~

Gwen swept through the door of the newspaper office. She didn't bother to greet everyone as she hurried to her desk and sat down. She wanted to write about the fire while it was still fresh in her mind.

She arranged her pen, ink, and paper on her desk, brought her notebook out, and glanced at her notes. In her mind's eye, she tried to remember everything, from the heat to the smoke to the hardworking men.

Taking the lid off the ink bottle, she dipped her pen, and tapped it on the rim. She began writing down the account, only marking out a few words here or there, editing as she went along. Quickly, she completed the article. She read back over it, making another revision or two, and set it aside.

On a fresh sheet of paper, she started the piece about the fountain. She wrote it in an affable manner, describing it as interestingly as she could and scanned it once to check for errors.

With everything completed, she gathered her papers and arose. She went to Mr. Jennings's desk and waited for him to look up.

"There was a fire at the Rock Island yards this afternoon." She handed him the papers. "And I finished the assignment about the humane fountain."

"Hmm." Mr. Jennings perused her endeavors. After a few moments, he peered up at her, took off his spectacles, and placed them carefully on the scattered papers on his desk. "You know, Gwen, your writing has improved a great deal since you began working here. You are concise yet descriptive. Well done." He placed her work in the tray.

She was almost overwhelmed by his compliment. After all this time, it was a huge boost to her confidence. "Thank you, sir."

"It's a shame you'll be leaving the *Globe* so soon."

"I will?" She was confused by his comment.

"Manning informed me the other night that you would be resigning in mid-June." He raised his eyebrows.

"Oh…yes…well," she stammered. "I didn't realize Walter had said anything."

"Yes. He did." He cleared his throat and returned his spectacles to his face. "You may go home for the day, if you'd like."

"Thank you, Mr. Jennings."

Gwen tried not to show any emotion as she went out the door. As soon as she was out of sight, she stormed down the sidewalk. With each step, she became more furious. What a humiliation! To have the man in your life tell your boss you were quitting! She couldn't believe Walter had done it. What irritated her the most was the fact that they hadn't even discussed a definite date for her departure yet. She had planned more on July or August.

Her paced slowed as she pondered the situation. She didn't know if she should say anything to Walter or not, because she hated confrontations. The damage was done anyway. She couldn't very well go back and tell Mr. Jennings that Walter was wrong. She would just have to accept that she would be leaving her family and dear friends in Shawnee in a few weeks—whether she liked it or not.

CHAPTER FOURTEEN

Gwen avoided Rose and Josh for the next several days. She wasn't sure why, but she knew she just wasn't ready to tell them how soon she was moving back to Guthrie. It was surprisingly easy not to spend time with Josh. Luke had brought him a load of lumber the night of the fire and Josh had spent every spare minute working on a project. He would update the women of the house every evening at supper how his chair was coming along. Just about everyone except Gwen had been out to see his work. She waited.

Walter continued to call frequently. They had talked a few times before he finally brought up her resignation. She was staring out the kitchen window, daydreaming about things she needed to get done, when she turned all her attention to Walter's words on the telephone.

"I've told Jennings you were moving back," he said.

"Yes?" She wasn't sure how to respond.

"I told him the fourteenth of June would be your final day."

"Yes. That's what he said." She decided to question him about it, but she did so cautiously. "I thought I had more time here."

He cleared his throat. "Logan's wife had their baby. I thought it was time for you to return and begin with wedding preparations.

Your mother agreed with me. She's quite anxious about your homecoming." He didn't precisely sound as if he was apologizing, but she knew it was as good as she would get.

"I'm sure she is. The last time I was there, she was fairly flustered that I hadn't picked out a style of wedding gown for the dressmaker yet."

"Yes, and, as I said, spare no expense. I'll cover any extraordinary costs," he said generously.

"Thank you, but really...something simple is what I would prefer."

"The wedding should be an extravagant affair. You should have all the lace and frills necessary. All my colleagues will be there," he insisted.

"Of course, Walter," she agreed. She didn't really care anyway. Besides, who wouldn't want to be the best-dressed bride in Guthrie?

She watched Josh stride out of the carriage house toward the kitchen. "I need to go, Walter," she said quickly. She hoped to leave the room before Josh came in.

"I'd like to solidify the matter, Gwendolyn. Your last day at the paper is the fourteenth. You will move back on the fifteenth. Is that our arrangement?" Walter asked.

Josh opened the back door and entered.

"Yes. That sounds good. I'll talk to you later. Good-bye." She hung up the earpiece and was afraid she did so before Walter said farewell.

Josh appeared to be waiting for her. He grinned and said, "I've just about finished the chair. Would you come out and see if it's nice enough to sell?"

"Well, I have some things to do..."

"It won't take long," he encouraged.

"Yes, for a moment."

He held the door for her and followed as she led the way across the yard. They went into the dim interior of the carriage house.

The half-wild cat that she had seen only glimpses of for the past two years was curled up on top of some old rags.

"I see you've made a friend," she commented.

"Aye. It's taken time and a lot of table scraps to get him to be sociable, but Mac is a good lad now."

Gwen chuckled before she spotted the new dining room chair that was placed on top of the workbench. She went up to it and studied it silently. It was beautiful. The seat was a solid piece of wood, slightly scooped out. The legs and spindles on the back were turned. The top piece of wood was a good twelve inches and was gently curved, and carved into it was a simple yet elegant scroll design. The workmanship was excellent.

"It just needs a couple coats of varnish, and I'll be done." He brushed off a speck of sawdust. "What do you think?"

"It's wonderful, Josh," she said at last. "You should be proud."

He nodded and smiled down at her. "I wish Granddad Flynn could see it. He's the one who had the love for wood. He taught me most of what I know."

"He would love it, I assure you." She gingerly touched the velvety-smooth chair that was like a work of art. "Speaking of your grandpa, I was wondering…"

"Aye?" He appeared curious.

"I've wanted to write a novel." She paused and then plunged into her explanation. "I've finally realized that if I researched a real event like a voyage across the sea that my writing would seem more…real. I was wondering if you or your family would mind if I expanded on some of your grandparents' immigration stories for my book."

"Honestly?" He seemed to be considering her request before he grinned. "I think we'd all be pleased to be considered worthy of such literary efforts. Just try to make us sound as wonderful as we are," he joked.

She smiled. "I didn't think you would mind, but I thought I should ask first." She was relieved. Now she could begin putting her efforts into research and writing her ideas down.

"I'll put my mind to it and see if I can remember anything else, if you'd like," he said helpfully.

"I would. Thanks."

"So how have you been? I haven't seen much of you lately," Josh asked as he leaned against the bench.

"Fine. Fine," she said lightly. She stood there awkwardly. This would be a perfect time to tell him she was moving, but she didn't want to do it. She wondered how she could leave gracefully. "I... uh...told Mrs. Brown I'd help her with something...I'd better go back in." She hated lying, but she really wanted to get away.

He nodded. "See you soon."

Gwen gave him what she hoped was a friendly smile and made haste out the door. As she hurried across the lawn, she couldn't figure out why she didn't want to tell him about her imminent departure. She only knew she wasn't ready. And, honestly, she didn't know how or when she *could* tell him.

~

One evening a few days later, Gwen was sitting in the parlor with a wooden box full of stereoscope cards. She was hoping for some more inspiration for her story and she knew she had some views of Europe as well as America among the cards. Finally, she came across the ones she was looking for. She pulled out several cards of Ireland.

She placed the first one in the stereoscope, put it to her eyes, and adjusted the distance until it was in focus. The photograph was of the Irish countryside, complete with rock walls. Others were of a thatched-roofed cottage, Dublin, and Galway.

She was so engrossed that she didn't notice Josh until he spoke.

"What do you have there?" he asked as he eased himself onto the sofa with the box between them.

"These are some views of Ireland. Look." She handed it to him. "Isn't it wonderful? It's almost as if you're there," she gushed.

"It is," he commented after he had repositioned it.

"I'd *love* to go there someday. It must be so lush and beautiful." She sighed, knowing she probably would never go to the place of her dreams.

"You act like it'll never happen." He lowered the stereoscope and scanned her face.

"I'm only being realistic. I probably won't ever be able to go." She shrugged.

"If your man knew, wouldn't he take you?"

"I don't think so," she said casually.

"If a body wanted to travel, he could save every cent until he had enough money." Josh seemed overly concerned about the subject.

"It's not the cost..." Gwen weighed how much she should divulge. "We've talked about it. Walter isn't one for travel abroad."

"Even when he knows how dearly you'd like to go?" he asked with his eyebrows drawn together.

She didn't answer. And she did not want to hear what he was insinuating.

"If I were to marry, I'd do whatever I could for my love," he said sincerely.

She began to gather her cards. She wasn't going to listen to him suggest Walter didn't love her enough.

"I'm sorry, Gwen." He placed a hand over hers. "I didn't mean to—"

"It's fine," she said tersely. She pulled her hand away from his.

A knock at the door saved them from an increasingly awkward situation. She hopped up as if her skirts were on fire and all but ran to the door. She opened it and found Owen standing there.

"Hello, Owen. How are you?" Gwen asked cheerfully as she let him in.

"I'm exceptional." He smiled as he took off his hat.

"Did Rose come with you?" she asked, peering over his shoulder.

"She went home after we closed to start supper, but I came by to tell Flynn something. Is he around?"

Gwen shut the door and turned to get Josh, but he had already emerged from the parlor. The men shook hands.

"I have some stupendous news, Flynn." Owen's voice was animated. "A wealthy spinster, Miss Duffy, came in the store today and absolutely admired the chair you made. She bought it on the spot."

"That is good news." Josh looked pleased.

"That's not all. She requested seven more chairs and a dining table to match. She said she would pay handsomely for it all."

"How wonderful," Gwen said enthusiastically. In spite of her recent irritation with Josh, she was happy for him. "It's quite a compliment."

"Aye. And quite a tall order." He raised his eyebrows. "She'll know it'll take time since I have another job?"

"Yes. From what I gather, she is in the process of having a big house built on Beard Street. She won't need it right away."

"Good." Josh grinned broadly and rubbed his hands together. "This is an interesting turn of events. I'll walk out with you and go over the details."

"Tell Rose I said hello," Gwen said as they went out.

She needed to talk with Mrs. Brown and knew that she definitely couldn't put that off any longer. She found her, as expected, in the kitchen tidying up.

"Mrs. Brown, I need to tell you something."

The older lady put a dish in a cupboard before turning and giving Gwen her full attention. "What's on yer mind?"

"I know it's short notice, but I need to move back to Guthrie on the fifteenth. The wedding date is closing in on me and I need to go home," Gwen said apologetically.

"I usually like more notice than this, but we've known from the start your stay was only temporary. As luck would have it, another gal was just in here yesterday asking for a room." Mrs.

Brown squeezed Gwen's shoulders. "It's been nice to have ya around fer so long. You're a good girl."

"Thank you." Gwen tried not to get emotional. "You've been like a second mother to me. I appreciate all you've done."

"Aw, weren't nothin'." She pushed a stray gray hair off the nape of her neck.

"I have a favor to ask also."

"What'd that be?"

"Can you not tell the others in the house that I'm moving? I thought I'd wait."

Mrs. Brown shrugged. "Whatever you think, darlin'. I'll not say a thing."

"I'd appreciate it," Gwen said with relief. "Now let me help you put those dishes away."

CHAPTER FIFTEEN

Josh was slow to wake. As he opened his eyes, he saw Gwen sitting at the table. Her head was down and she was scribbling with a pencil on some paper. She looked so happy and content. He tried to speak to her but, curiously, no words would flow. She must have seen him stir, because she glanced up and gave him the sweetest smile—a smile that was meant only for him. He reached out for her, but she began to fade. It felt as if he were falling into the black night.

"No!"

Josh's shout echoed in the empty room. He bolted upright in bed. His eyes searched furiously. He was alone. It had all been a dream.

The faint light from the windows showed that it was almost dawn. He flopped back down. His heart was pounding, and he was sweating. Sleep would elude him now.

He wanted desperately to recapture the good part of the dream. When Gwen smiled at him, it made him feel as if he were the happiest man on earth. As the gravity of his situation hit him, he groaned. Feelings like these wouldn't be there unless he truly cared for Gwen. He stared at the crack in the ceiling. He loved her. He knew it. He had probably known it for a while but hadn't admitted it to himself because of her man. Walter Manning. He wanted to curse the name.

Until he met Manning, he couldn't begrudge the fact that Gwen was going to be married soon. But after trying to talk to Manning and finding out what type of man he was, Josh's stomach wanted to twist up. He did not like Walter Manning. He didn't understand why Gwen did. The worst thing was that he didn't know what he was going to do about it.

~

"Well, we knew the time had to come someday." Rose gave a bittersweet sigh as she responded to Gwen's news. "This will be our last Sunday afternoon on my porch sharing a glass of tea." Rose clinked her glass against Gwen's.

"Don't say that. I'll be back. Maybe not often…" Gwen began, knowing full well that Walter probably wouldn't like her to travel back and forth alone after they were married. She wouldn't think of that right now.

Gwen sipped her drink. She wanted to soak in the serenity of spending time with her dearest friend while Owen was entertaining Hope in the parlor. The day was warm, but not oppressive, and the wind helped keep them cool. A crow cawed noisily from a branch in a tree while a squirrel chattered angrily in return as if it wanted the crow to leave his home. She smiled and turned her gaze to Rose.

"I'll miss you," Gwen stated simply.

Rose nodded. "I feel the same."

"But you'll still come and sing at my wedding. We'll have that time together." Gwen brightened.

"As my grandma used to say, 'God willin' and the creeks don't rise.' I'll be there." Rose's lips turned up.

"Good. I couldn't bear it if you and Ada weren't there. Besides my family, you two are the most important people on my invitation list."

Rose nodded. "I guess you've told Ada and Luke?"

"Yes. I rented a rig and drove out there yesterday. You should see how Lucy has grown!" She paused as she remembered her visit. "Luke and Ada were both quiet about my announcement. Luke especially."

"I could see how he would be upset about it. You're like a sister to him," Rose observed. "What about Josh?" she asked in a guarded manner.

"Oh, I'll tell him soon." She waved her hand nonchalantly.

"How do you feel about leaving him so soon after your renewed friendship?"

"Oh…" Gwen was taken aback by the question. "Well, you know…It has been good to see him again, but it's time I head back to Guthrie and get ready for my wedding," she finished confidently.

"It's probably for the best," Rose said quietly.

"Why do you say that?" Gwen asked.

Rose pondered the question for a moment before she said, "It's nothing, Gwen, honestly."

Gwen thought about pressing her, but decided against it. It really wasn't important. At least Gwen hoped so.

~

Josh whistled an Irish jig as he carried his newest chair into the Emersons' store. Rose was helping a statuesque older lady at the counter. Owen quickly emerged from the back room.

"Hello, Flynn," he greeted.

The customer turned to look at Josh. He gave the lady a friendly smile and tipped his cap to her. She had soft features and kind, pale eyes. Her hair was the purest shade of white, and she wore a fashionable light-blue hat and dress.

Owen escorted the lady toward Josh. "Flynn. I'd like you to meet Miss Cordelia Duffy."

Miss Duffy extended her hand. Josh quickly deposited the chair on the floor, wiped his sweaty fingers on his trousers, and took her hand in a firm handshake.

"Mr. Flynn. I had to meet the artisan that produced such beautiful furniture," Miss Duffy said in a soft voice that hinted of their mutual ancestral home.

"Thank you, ma'am. I'm glad you like it." Josh was impressed that someone of such obvious upscale social standing would even think of personally meeting with him.

"Mrs. Emerson was kind enough to telephone me and tell me you were on your way here. I've settled my account—do you mind putting your lovely chair in my buggy?"

"Of course I don't mind."

He picked up the chair as Miss Duffy bid the Emersons farewell. He held the door for her as she led the way to a fine horse and buggy. He put the chair in the buggy for her.

"Where do you hail from, Mr. Flynn?" she asked in a personable way.

"I've lived in Kansas and even Guthrie for a time. But my grandparents were from County Kerry. "

"What brings you to Shawnee?" she asked with a twinkle in her eye. "Any skeletons in the closet that you're running from?"

Josh chuckled. "No, ma'am. I work in the cabinet shops for the Rock Island."

She nodded as if she were deliberating about something. "I have a proposition for you, my lad."

"Aye?"

"I'm having a house built. My foreman, who was living on the site, was not up to par and I had to let him go. I was wondering if, along with completing the dining set, you would be my new foreman and straighten out the entire mess."

"Oh, I don't know, ma'am. I've never done anything like that before." He was astonished by her offer.

"I would pay you handsomely and you could live on-site, above the carriage house, rent free," she proposed.

"I don't—"

"Will you accompany me over there and take a look at the place before you decide?"

Josh shrugged. "I don't see why not." He might as well consider her offer.

He helped her up, untied the lead rope from the ring in the sidewalk, and climbed in. She took the reins, released the brake, and set the black mare in motion. They went quite a few blocks—there weren't many homes that far out. She pulled over at a large construction site on the east side of the road.

As she had said, the carriage house out back was completed and painted yellow with white trim. It faced the south, giving better light than where he currently lived. The house was positioned with the front door looking toward Beard Street. The framing was complete, and the house appeared to be three stories tall. Floor joists were in place and doorways and windows framed out, but nothing else was done. Lumber was scattered carelessly around the yard.

"What do you think, Mr. Flynn?" she asked as she surveyed the skeleton of her new home.

"It's a big job."

"Yes, it is. The third floor will be the servants' quarters. The house will have all the modern conveniences."

Josh mused over the enormity of the project.

"I would also like you to carve original mantelpieces for the four fireplaces and any other delicate woodworking."

He just wasn't sure he would know how to manage the construction of such a grand house.

"All the carpenters will remain. Some are quite experienced, but I wasn't sure if they were up to the task of foreman." Miss Duffy turned toward him and looked him in the eyes. "The Emersons have been kind enough to recommend you. And I'm a fairly good judge of character. I believe what you lack in experience you will more than make up for with perseverance. What do you say?"

"I truly appreciate your confidence in me, Miss Duffy. But how can I quit my job for one that I might not be good at?"

"If things don't work out, I'll talk to all my friends about purchasing furniture from you. I believe you have a bright future ahead of you, my lad."

He was in awe. No stranger had ever been so considerate to him. "I'm still not sure."

"Take time to think it over," she insisted.

He thought that was a bonny idea. "I will."

"I'll give you one week to decide." She smiled as if she were glad he didn't say no right away. "You can telephone me at number one-three-three. Let me know either way."

"I will, Miss Duffy. I surely will."

CHAPTER SIXTEEN

Josh closed the fat book he had been reading with a thump and left it on the table as he stood up to stretch. He had found a book at the library about constructing houses. He wanted to make as informed a decision as he could and he didn't want to turn down or accept Miss Duffy's offer until he felt completely confident about it.

A knock at the door surprised him. No one ever ventured up to his place. He opened the door, expecting his visitor to be Mrs. Brown. Instead, Gwen was standing there.

"This is unexpected. Come on in if you don't think Mrs. Brown will have a fit," he joked.

She smiled. "I told her ahead of time. She said I could come as long as we keep the door open."

"Then by all means, enter." He bowed and swept his arm toward his humble abode.

He offered her a chair, but she shook her head.

"So what brings you here?" he asked.

Gwen's fingers were interlaced and now she squeezed them as if she were nervous. Her lips turned up, but there was no real humor in her expression. "I've come to tell you that I'm moving back to Guthrie on Saturday," she said, attempting to sound lighthearted.

The information hit him in the gut like a thunderbolt. She couldn't. Not now.

She turned as if she had completed her task.

"Saturday? So soon? Why?" he sputtered.

"It's time for me to return," she said simply.

"You can't. I—" He knew he sounded frantic.

She held up a hand. "Please, don't say anything that will make this more difficult. I'm really glad we rekindled our old friendship, but it's time for me to move back and marry Walter."

"You can't marry him," he said recklessly. "He's pompous and full of himself."

"How can you say that?" she asked indignantly. "You only met him once."

"I know, but…" He didn't know if he should say it or not, but he felt he would regret it for the rest of his life if he didn't. "I adore you, Gwen. I always have. You've become such a lovely woman. Everything about you is grace and beauty."

"Ha! Now I know you're only jesting," she said heatedly. "There's not a graceful bone in my body."

"That's not how I see you," he said urgently.

His heart pounded in his ears. He felt as if he couldn't breathe. Why wouldn't she listen? All those wasted years washed over him in a torrent of fervent emotions. He grabbed her upper arms, pulled her to him, and kissed her with all the intensity he felt for her. He thought he felt a glimmer of response from her before she shoved him away.

She appeared horrified as she held the back of her shaking hand to her ruby lips.

"Did he ever kiss you like that?" he muttered gruffly.

"How dare you? How dare you! How could you do this to me now?" Her hands clenched as if she were ready for a fight. "I waited for you for *years*, Joshua Flynn! When we moved back to Guthrie

I would sit at my window and pine for you. At sixteen, eighteen, nineteen, I waited, hoping to see you coming down the walkway. I only got my first job at a newspaper in Guthrie to bide my time. Finally I gave up. I let my mother introduce me to Walter."

"I thought you didn't want me, Gwen! That's what I thought all these years. But after I was in the train wreck, I knew I had to find you again. I had to see if you cared at all..."

She was still visibly angry but she continued to listen.

"I moved back to Oklahoma Territory, and I was going to search every city and village, but our paths crossed on the train. Surely you feel as I do, and I was meant to find you. We're meant to be together."

"It's too late, Josh. You are too late."

"It's not too late!" he argued. "You're not married yet. Marry me, Gwen. Not him."

"I can't." Her shoulders slumped and she looked defeated. Silence stretched between them.

"I'll love you like he never could," he said gently.

"I can't." Tears welled in her eyes. "I *won't* cancel my wedding to Walter." She turned on her heel and started for the door.

"No! Stay!" He grasped her forearm. "I *can't* let you go!"

Gwen didn't say a word. She glanced down at his hand clutching her arm. He released her. He would never hurt her.

She held her head high and started down the stairs with dignity. About halfway, she began to hurry, and her boots pounded the boards. She broke into a run across the yard. The screen to the back door banged as she rushed into the boardinghouse.

Josh gently closed his door. He placed each palm on the smooth wood and leaned against it, his head hanging down. He didn't know how to fix this. He knew from his long search for love that no one compared to Gwen. If she wouldn't return his love, he knew he would be a changed man forever.

~

Gwen lay curled up in a ball on top of the bedspread. She wanted to hide in the sanctuary of her room for eternity. She dried her tears with a soggy handkerchief. She couldn't believe Josh had done that. How dare he kiss her in that way? No man had ever been so familiar with her. Walter had always been a perfect gentleman in her presence.

Someone rapped on the door. She stayed still, barely breathing. Surely Josh wouldn't have the audacity to come upstairs?

"Gwen? Are you in there?" Ada's voice was muffled.

"We came for coffee one last time," Rose added.

Gwen took a deep breath to clear her head. She slid off the bed, dabbed her eyes again, and blew her nose. After stashing the crumpled hankie in the top drawer of her bureau, she forced a smile and opened the door.

Ada and Rose were full of enthusiastic greetings until they saw her face.

"What's wrong?" Ada asked with complete concern.

"What happened?" Rose asked as she shut the door behind them.

"I really don't feel like talking about it right now," Gwen said as she sat on the chair at her desk.

Ada and Rose sat on the edge of her rumpled bed.

"If you don't want to confide in us, we understand," Rose offered.

"It's not that…I'm just so upset…I'm not sure I can say it."

They were silent as the battle waged in Gwen's brain. She finally gave in and decided to tell them the entire horrifying scene in hopes they could help her make sense of it all.

After she told them every maddening detail, she waited for their response.

Ada softly cleared her throat. Rose fiddled with the lace on the cuff of her pale-pink shirtwaist.

"How do you feel about it?" Ada asked.

"I would think it was obvious. I'm angry and appalled he would do such a thing. I'm on the cusp of my wedding to Walter. It's so rude and insulting. As if I would be so dishonorable as to leave Walter and marry him," she fumed.

Ada and Rose exchanged a knowing glance.

Rose finally asked carefully, "Which is more honorable? To marry someone you love or someone you don't?"

"Exactly!" Gwen agreed. She was beginning to perk up. "I love Walter, so I'll marry him as planned. This little…disturbance… will not affect a thing."

"So you have no qualms about marrying Walter?" Ada inquired.

"Of course I don't." Gwen hopped up. "I should have known a talk with my best friends would help. Let's go down, have some coffee, and see if Mrs. Brown has anything sweet to eat."

Gwen started downstairs. Right away she noticed a banner made from butcher paper over the parlor doorway. It said, *Farewell Gwen. We shall miss you!*

"Did you two know about this?" Gwen asked over her shoulder.

They nodded and grinned.

"We meant to keep you occupied for a few minutes while they decorated," Ada told her.

Gwen chuckled. She was the one who had kept them entertained. She hurried into the parlor to find it full of guests. Everyone shouted salutations. She couldn't believe how many people were there. Besides the other occupants of the house, Sister Mary Louise and several ladies from church were there. Luke, Owen, Mrs. Dennis, and the babies were accounted for. Even Mr. Jennings, Mr. Spitzer, and Mr. Abrams were present. The notable missing person was Josh, and she was glad. She was still miffed at him and wasn't up to seeing him yet.

Rose leaned close and whispered as if reading her mind, "We didn't invite Josh ahead of time. We assumed we could go get him when the time came. We weren't sure if you had told him your plans or not."

Gwen patted Rose's arm. "You did the best thing possible."

Luke cleared his throat loudly. "Ada and Rose put together this impromptu party for you, Gwen. They wanted you to know how much you will be missed." He held up a coffee mug. "To you, Gwen, may you always be healthy and happy. Cheers!"

Everyone held up their cups and echoed Luke's sentiments.

Mr. Jennings and her coworkers came forward as everyone else began to mingle. Mr. Jennings gave her a small oblong wooden box.

"We wanted you to have a little token to show how much we appreciate all you did at the *Globe*," Mr. Jennings said.

She lifted the hinged lid. Nestled in the red silk lining was a gold filigreed pen.

"It's lovely. Thank you. I enjoyed working there. Thank you for the opportunity," Gwen told him.

Mr. Jennings nodded. He glanced at the mantel clock. "We have to return to the office and finish some things."

"Thank you for coming, Mr. Jennings."

"Keep writing," he said as he made his way toward the door.

Mr. Spitzer and Mr. Abrams mumbled their goodwill wishes as they tipped their bowlers and followed Mr. Jennings out.

It meant a lot to Gwen that they took the time to come. She wished she had known she held their respect before now. It would have made her work experience all the more enjoyable. She wasn't one to hold a grudge, though, so she would try to remember them all fondly.

She gave a little internal sigh as she turned back to the party. It was amazing to have all the people she cared for the most here to bid her farewell. Eager to reminisce over fun times and talk about her future prospects, she wouldn't let the difficult emotions surrounding Josh cloud her evening. She wanted to have fun because she knew she would remember this night for the rest of her life.

~

Josh let the curtain drop. All the lights were still on at the boardinghouse. He had seen people arriving earlier and had guessed it was some kind of party for Gwen when he saw the men she worked with. He wondered why he hadn't been invited, but he was certain he wouldn't be wanted there now.

He knew he had been terribly inappropriate earlier, and while he felt a twinge of guilt for his behavior, he didn't think he had made a mistake about the things he had said or done. Truth be told, his impulsive behavior only made him want her more. He wanted to hold her in his arms, cherish her, and show her how much he loved her. He wasn't ready to let her go and he couldn't face the fact that she would soon be in the arms of another forever.

He decided to turn in. Gwen usually filled his dreams in one way or another. He began to look forward to his imaginings. It didn't seem as wrong when his mind conjured up visions of Gwen while he was sleeping.

He got under the covers, but soon kicked off the sheets. Turning from his back to his side, he stared at the curtain fluttering in the breeze. He replayed the last moments with Gwen over and over until his eyes finally closed and he was able to doze.

~

Gwen was standing in a green meadow as she smiled at him. It was so good to see her happy again. Josh ambled toward her with his hands in his pockets.

"I'm waiting," she said with a gentle lilt in her voice.

She held her hand out to him. He quickened his pace and reached for her. A man walked past him. Before he could respond, the blond man took her by the hand and led her away. She appeared confused.

"Don't leave me alone!" Josh shouted as they disappeared into a fog. "Gwen!"

Josh's eyes snapped open. His temple throbbed as he stared into the darkness. He groaned. Maybe it wasn't such a good idea to dream about Gwen after all. A tortured man would never get enough rest.

CHAPTER SEVENTEEN

The big day had finally arrived. Gwen was standing on the walkway in front of the boardinghouse in her brown traveling suit, with gloves buttoned, handbag on her arm, and hat secured. Her trunks and tan leather suitcases were stacked in the grass while she awaited the arrival of the hired man who was coming to take her and her things to the station.

She turned to take one last look at the house that had been her home for over two years. It hadn't been fancy accommodations by any means, but she'd had fun there. She had arrived little more than a girl and was leaving a gracious, although not quite elegant, lady.

She swiveled around and glimpsed Josh coming around the corner of the house. Her first impulse was to run away, but she stood her ground.

Josh came closer and stopped in front of her at a reasonable distance. "'Tis time, aye?" he commented as he glanced at her things on the lawn.

"Yes."

"I wanted to apologize for the other night. I—"

She held up her hand to stop him. "I'm not one to hold a grudge, Josh. I forgive you." She really did not want to drag the whole thing out into the light.

"Good." He paused, and his dark-brown eyes held hers. "I wanted to tell you if you change your mind about Manning or me—"

"Josh," she said sternly.

"I know it's improbable, but I want you to know that I'll always care for you. All you have to do is say the word and I'll come to you."

She didn't want to hear his tender words. She almost felt sorry for him. Almost. "Josh, don't be silly. You're not the type of man to yearn for a woman the rest of your life. You'll find someone, probably before my train pulls out of the station. I'm sure Bevin is more than willing."

"That's what you think of me? That I'm some kind of philanderer?" He appeared injured.

"I guess not. But how am I supposed to know? You could have changed in these many years," she replied.

He looked as if he was going to be angry, but then his features softened. "Do you remember when you were about to move from Guthrie? I came to your yard the night before you were to leave. You snuck out, and we shared our hopes and dreams for the future. We held each other in that awkward way that youngsters do, and I vowed we would be together again?"

"Of course I remember," she said crossly. She remembered every vivid detail. She would never forget the bright full moon, the dog barking in the neighborhood, or their first innocent kiss.

"I may have courted a few young ladies, but they never compared to you. They never measured up. I never forgot my vow and told Granny about it one day. She was the one who told me not long ago that I'd never be happy unless I fulfilled that promise and found you again."

"And so you did, but it's too late."

He nodded slowly. "I wasted too much time."

"Yes. You did," she agreed. She didn't understand why he was burdening her with all this. "But I *am* getting married in a few months. You will move on and be fine in no time."

"Maybe, but until I know you've said 'I do,' I won't give up hope that you'll have a change of heart."

"Josh." She sighed in exasperation. "I would never dishonor myself or my family in such a way."

"Dishonor? That's all you say about it? No cries of undying love for him? No words of passion for your beloved? You only worry about what the neighbors think?" He raised his eyebrows.

"Of course I love him!" She was getting irritated and tired of this conversation. She twirled away from him.

He was silent for so long she thought maybe he had slipped away.

"I made something for you," he said quietly from behind her back.

Curiosity won out over indignation. She turned around. He held up his palm. A small, intricately carved wooden Celtic cross lay in his hand. The base was about four inches square and the cross itself was about four inches tall.

"Oh, Josh." She really was speechless. She didn't know if she should accept it or not.

"From one old friend to another?" He placed it in her gloved hand.

She rotated it as she admired it. The sharp aroma of cedar wafted up as she looked at the carved Celtic knots. She saw his monogram of an intertwined *J* and *F* carved into the bottom.

"Thank you," she said softly.

A wagon rattled up the street and stopped next to them.

"It looks as if your ride is here," he said reluctantly.

"Yes."

Between the three of them, her items were loaded quickly. The driver hopped up into the seat. Josh helped her climb up. He held her hand for a moment and squeezed it longer than Gwen thought was necessary.

"Good-bye, Gwen," he said gently as he peered up at her.

"Good-bye." She was startled by the lump in her throat and the tears that sprang into her eyes. She pulled her hand away. "I'm ready to go, sir," she informed the driver.

She did not look back as they drove away. Removing her little handbag from her arm, she fumbled to get it open. She took a handkerchief out and placed the cross inside. After they turned the corner, she dabbed her eyes. Taking a deep breath, she straightened her shoulders. She would be so glad when the day was over and she was finally in Guthrie.

~

Gwen stepped off the train at Union Station. She searched for her family or Walter. She couldn't see anyone and was beginning to conclude they had all forgotten her when she saw her gangly brothers waving madly. The twins were all arms and legs. Appendages flew in every direction as they ran toward her. They skidded to a stop in front of her.

"Hey, sis," they said in unison. Their boyish voices were beginning to crack as they matured.

"How are my boys?" Gwen asked with a grin.

George and Gilbert gave her dignified hugs before elbowing each other and knocking their navy-blue caps askew. The boys were not identical twins. They had a similar appearance—brown hair and eyes—but serious George's hair was straight and orderly while Gilbert was as carefree as his ever-wayward hair.

"Mom had a cake in the oven," George began.

"And Walter needed to stay late at the office," Gilbert added.

"So they sent us to fetch you," George finished.

"Well, I couldn't ask for better escorts," Gwen said with a smile.

They went with her as she arranged for someone to get her luggage. Once everything was loaded, the boys perched precariously on top of her trunks while she rode up front. She constantly glanced back to make sure they didn't fall off and break their necks as they went up the steep hill on Oklahoma Avenue. The driver turned off the busy downtown street to Broad Street, turned east on Cleveland Avenue, and soon stopped in front of their home.

The two-story white colonial revival-style house with thick porch columns had been their home since they returned to Guthrie. Luke's father had scouted out the place, which was down the street from his own home. After Gwen's mother had given her quick approval, the house had been purchased with inheritance money from the estate of Gwen's grandparents.

Gwen's items were unloaded, and her brothers dragged, pushed, and pulled her heavy trunks through the front door, making entirely too much racket. Her mother came down the hallway next to the wide, open stairway with a towel in her hand.

"My goodness. A person would think a herd of horses had stampeded through the foyer from all that commotion," her mother, Grace, said. "Leave them there for now, boys, before you ruin the parquet floors. We'll get them upstairs presently."

Her mother appeared calm and refined as usual in a dark-plum dress with ecru lace at the neck and wrists. Gwen had always been told she looked like her mother. They had the same coloring, only her mother was graying at the temples. She could only hope she would look that cool after baking in the hot kitchen.

Her mother hugged Gwen quickly and pecked her cheek. "You look well, Gwendolyn. I'm glad you're home at last."

"I am too," Gwen agreed as she removed her hat and gloves and placed them on the large walnut hall tree.

Their heels clicked on the shiny floors as they walked. They bypassed the study on the right, Gwen's favorite room. It had a plush green-and-white oriental rug, two comfortable red-and-green floral tufted armchairs at one side of the floor-to-ceiling windows, and a desk at the other side. The southern exposure ensured the room was always bright. The walls were lined with books and more books. She shared this passion with her mother, who had collected them for years. There were books about history, science, and the arts, and plenty of novels lining the shelves.

Her mother had tutored Gwen at home when they lived on the farm too far from a school. Gwen had continued her education at home wherever they lived until it became too much for her mother to watch twin boys and help Gwen. Gwen went reluctantly to high school in Guthrie. She did well academically and made friends, but she missed her days of curling up in the study with a good book most of the day.

They went through the plush parlor with its tapestry-upholstered sofa and armchairs and heavy draperies in dark green and burgundy.

"It smells good in here," Gwen commented as they neared the kitchen at the back of the house.

"I made your favorite spice cake."

"Yum. I'm famished." She spied the cake on the formal dining room table. She breathed in the aroma and swiped the sugar glaze with a finger to taste it.

"Now, now. You know better," her mother reprimanded kindly as she went into the kitchen.

Gwen stepped over to the sideboard and took out the white-and-red oriental-inspired plates, a knife, and some silverware. Her brothers hovered nearby eyeing the special treat. Their mother returned with cups of coffee and milk on a black-enameled tray. They all sat around the table.

"Walter said he would stop by after work," her mother informed her.

"Oh, good. Is Pa coming home this weekend?" Gwen asked.

"Not this one but next," her mother said before placing a slice of cake on Gilbert's plate.

Gwen nodded. Her father was the foreman for the crew that helped the surveyors establish new routes for the Santa Fe. His time at home was always too short.

"We have so many things to do now that you're home. We need to decide on invitations, choose the baker, and have fittings for your new gown," her mother began.

"Fittings? I haven't even chosen a pattern yet." Gwen took a bite of the dense cake.

Her mother appeared almost apologetic. "You kept putting it off, dear, and if we wanted the best in town a decision had to be made. I took some prints of gowns to Walter and we chose one. Miss Randolph agreed that it was quite lovely."

"Mother." Gwen was shocked that her mother would do such a thing and more than a little irritated that Tina had been consulted at all. But what was important was that Walter approved. "So Walter liked it?"

"Oh yes. He said he'd be proud to see you coming down the aisle in this design," her mother reassured her.

"Well…"

"It had to be done, dear. I took one of your evening gowns over for the measurements. The pale-pink one with the ink stain? Madame Lorraine already has your wedding gown ready for you to try on. I'm sure if you have any definite objections to the style, she can make some slight alterations. She is the best, you know."

Gwen's first reaction was to be irritated, but she seriously hadn't had a design in mind. If it was one thing she didn't have to do so she could spend time writing, she couldn't be too angry. After all, writing her book was the one thing that *she* wanted to do most before she got married.

CHAPTER EIGHTEEN

True to her word, Gwen's mother kept her busy the following week. They visited a printer, a baker, and, of course, Madame Lorraine's establishment on Harrison Avenue. The seamstress shop was on the bottom floor of a two-story redbrick building with huge plate-glass windows. It was a typical shop of that sort with rows and rows of bolts of material and examples of outfits.

Madame Lorraine was a rather large but meticulously dressed middle-aged woman with an amazing amount of black hair piled on the top of her head. She had a no-nonsense demeanor and was extremely professional and wonderfully talented.

In a back room, Madame Lorraine personally helped Gwen into the basted gown. As the seamstress extraordinaire fussed over the dress, checking the size and fit, Gwen studied herself in the tall mirror. The gown was of white silk with a terribly long train. The sleeves had such big puffs at the shoulders Gwen was afraid she would have to walk through the doors of the church sideways. There were hundreds of tucks in the loosely fitted bodice, and the wide, lace-covered neck was stiff and boned. The entire concoction was covered with soft, filmy voile. She felt as if her head was poking out of a scratchy cloud. It was a couture dress to be sure. She admired the workmanship. She only wished she loved it.

"What do you think, mademoiselle?"

"It's beautifully made," Gwen answered honestly.

"Yes. We are the best in the territory," Madame Lorraine said confidently as she peered at Gwen's face in the mirror. "The style? How is the style for you?"

"Well…" Gwen began. She almost decided not to say anything because her parents were paying for the extravagance, but it was her wedding after all. "I would prefer not to have all this on." She fingered the voile. "Maybe it could be removed and made into a veil?"

Madame Lorraine seemed to be considering what she was saying.

"Also…the sleeves. Could they be a little less…puffy?" Gwen asked.

The seamstress remained silent.

"And I would like the train to be at least half as long."

Madame Lorraine glanced heavenward for a moment before she put a patient smile on her face. "It will cost extra to redo what has already been done."

"I understand. I'll pay the difference myself," Gwen assured her.

Madame Lorraine nodded slowly. "I will do it." She began to check the length and muttered, "I told your mother it was best for the *bride* to select the gown, *not* the mother."

"Oh, and could you not mention it to her? I will explain it all later."

"I will do as you wish, mademoiselle."

∼

A few days after Gwen left, Josh was leaving work after his shift when Thompson popped around the corner and began to follow on Josh's heels like a mongrel dog.

"What's your hurry, old chap? Going to meet your lady love?"

"No," Josh said tersely.

Thompson jumped in front of Josh, making him stumble to a stop. "What's the matter, Flynn? Did the lady tire of looking at that Irish ape of a face?"

"Get out of my way," Josh said through gritted teeth.

"It's for the best, you know," Thompson gloated. "You Irish should keep to your own kind and leave us civilized folks alone."

Josh was tired of Thompson's mouth. He clenched his fist. He wanted to shut him up once and for all. "You're right, Thompson."

Thompson's jaw dropped.

"We Irish *are* only mindless beasts. So you shouldn't be surprised when I do this—" Josh reared his arm back and punched Thompson square in the nose.

Thompson fell flat on his rump. His trembling hand touched his trickling nose. "I'm bleeding." His eyes were as wide as saucers. "I'm bleeding!" he blubbered. He wasn't as bold as his words after all.

"Flynn!" Mr. Miller shouted from over Josh's shoulder. He stomped toward them. "I told you—"

Josh shook his right hand to work out the twinge of pain in his fingers. "I know, sir." Josh turned to his boss. "You don't have to fire me. I quit."

Josh walked away with his head held high. He was glad his decision had been practically made for him. He would go straight away and telephone Miss Duffy. He was ready for a change. Maybe this would be the thing to get his mind off his troubles.

~

Gwen was deeply involved reading an account about the Irish famine from a book she had found in the study when she heard a queer noise. She looked up from the paper where she was making notations for reference. She got up from the desk and went to the window. Parked out front was a shiny tan automobile. The man behind the driving cap, goggles, and long brown overcoat was Walter. He descended the contraption and strode proudly toward the house.

Gwen hurried outside. She couldn't believe he had actually bought it. Automobiles were so expensive.

"You did it." It was the only thing she could think to say.

"I did." It was strange to see Walter beaming so. "The man drove it up today. What do you think?"

"It's a wonder, that's for sure."

"I'll take you for a ride."

"Right now?"

"Why not?" he asked.

"Do you know how to drive it?" she asked uncertainly.

"Yes, Gwendolyn. Now come along. I have another surprise for you."

He took her by the elbow and escorted her down the walkway. She glanced back, thinking she ought to tell her mother she was leaving. Her mother waved from the parlor window.

"Wait. I need my hat," Gwen said.

"That is taken care of." Walter smiled. He bent and reached onto the floor of the rear seat and produced a woman's hat with voluminous veiling.

While she was trying to secure it to her hair with the provided hat pins, he held up a long, thin, canvas-type overcoat and helped her into it. She tried to anchor the veiling as best she could and stepped up into the vehicle and sat in the tufted black leather seat.

She was getting warm in her getup as Walter went around to the front of the automobile and cranked the handle until it sputtered to life. He hopped in, and before she could hold on, they were off. The long metal rod with something that resembled a wheel was used to steer the horseless carriage.

Gwen actually could appreciate the innovation, but after smelling the fuel and careening around a couple of corners at an unsuitable amount of speed, she began to feel queasy.

"Where are we going?" she shouted over the wind and motor noise.

"We will be there momentarily." He seemed to be thoroughly enjoying himself.

Not soon enough for Gwen, they stopped in front of a square, two-story tan brick house with white trim on Vilas Avenue. She lifted the veil and piled it on top of her hat.

Once the vehicle was turned off, Walter removed his goggles, dug into his vest pocket, and produced a key. He placed it in her hand.

"*This* is our new home," Walter announced. "I closed on the sale yesterday. It's only a starter house, mind you. I expect my prospects to only improve after statehood."

Gwen swallowed hard. She wished the ride hadn't made her stomach so unsettled. She had assumed they would look for a house together. This one was farther away from St. Mary's church than she would have liked, but it *was* closer to Walter's work. She decided quickly it was best to be flattered that her fiancé would care enough to choose a house for them.

"It's nice, Walter," she finally said.

"I thought so. When Miss Randolph saw the advertisement in the newspaper, I knew I needed to look at it. I thought it was ideal for us. I wanted to surprise you."

"You certainly did."

He helped her down, and they went up the brick walkway. He showed her the house in short order. It was an unadorned type of house without fancy moldings or woodwork. All the walls in the square rooms were painted white. It was uninspiring to her when she felt she should be seeing it as a blank canvas ready to be decorated.

Of course she didn't share her feelings with Walter. She knew he was happy with the house. Her mind was probably just too full of characters, scenes, and plots to be interested in another creative outlet. Anyway, she had several months to mull over decorating options and get some inspiration.

~

The grandfather clock in the parlor chimed nine o'clock. Gwen's mother was darning a sock. George and Gilbert were playing chess at the game table in the corner. Gwen was lounging on the sofa, pencil and notepad in hand, trying to decide on names for the main characters in her story.

The front door rattled. They all glanced up curiously.

"Hallo there! Anyone home?" Gwen's father's voice boomed from the entryway.

"Pop!" the twins shouted.

Everyone jumped up and rushed to him. He was quickly bombarded with kisses, hugs, and handshakes. He chuckled heartily at his reception.

Her father looked the same as always with his thick gray hair and dear old muttonchops. His broad shoulders and barrel chest stretched his worn black traveling suit.

"How are one and all?" her father asked amid the commotion. After everyone gave a satisfactory answer, he dug around in his coat pocket and pulled out a small orange book. "Who would like the latest adventures of Kit Carson?"

"Oh boy!" George grinned from ear to ear.

"That's swell, Pop!" Gilbert said as he took the dime novel. "Let's go up and read it now, George."

"You couldn't stop me."

They raced up the stairs and remembered their manners about halfway up. "Thanks, Pop!" they called out together.

Her father squeezed Gwen's shoulders again. "Sorry I didn't bring my dear daughter a trinket."

"You know I don't care anything about that," Gwen said as they walked toward the parlor.

"Do you need anything to eat or drink, dear?" her mother asked.

"I'm fine for now," her father replied.

Her mother went to her chair and resumed her mending. Her father sat in his customary chair next to his wife. Gwen plopped back down on the sofa.

"Your posture, dear," her mother advised without even looking up.

Gwen dutifully sat up straight without her back touching the back of the sofa.

"Your mother wrote to say you were returning to us for a few months before the long-awaited occasion of your wedding," he commented with a smile.

"Yes."

"Are you excited the date is finally set?" he asked with a twinkle in his eye.

"Of course." Gwen chuckled.

"Anything exciting happen since I saw you last?" he asked offhandedly.

Gwen thought for a moment. "Do you remember a family named Flynn? I was friends with their boy, Josh."

"Yes. Yes. I remember them. They were a nice family. Seems like the father was a carpenter," her father said.

Gwen nodded. "Josh showed up in Shawnee not long ago. It was fun to see him again."

Her mother looked up quickly, something akin to alarm in her expression.

Her father smiled fondly as if he were remembering something. "Did you ever know there were two reasons why we moved from Guthrie?"

Gwen shrugged. "I always thought it was because of your job."

"It was that, but the impetus was that your mother wanted to get you away from that boy." He grinned.

"Josh?" Gwen was astonished. She looked to her mother for some kind of explanation.

"You were spending entirely too much time over there and you were becoming far too attached to that Irish boy." Her mother went back to her task, insinuating that the conversation was laid to rest.

That comment irritated Gwen. She wasn't usually disrespectful to her mother, but she could not stop herself from asking, "Was it alarming because he was a boy or because he was Irish?"

Her mother stared at her sternly. "Honestly, Gwen. Your impertinence amazes me. You know as well as I do that his prospects for the future were dim. No one would hire him for more than a common laborer. We wanted better for you than that."

"No one thinks like that anymore, Mother!" Gwen exclaimed. Her dander was up now. "Besides, Pa was a farmer. He worked with his hands. He still does."

"We *dallied* with farming because we had the resources to try such a thing. As to his current position, you know he is an important supervisor over a large crew of men."

"Now, ladies, let's not have a tussle." Her father stood and held his hand out to her mother. "I think I'm ready for a bite of something after all. Would you care to join us, Gwen?"

"No. I'm not hungry. I think I'll turn in early."

Her mother came to her. She kissed her cheek and whispered, "We did it for you. For your future. Good night, dear."

Gwen watched her parents stroll toward the kitchen. She was still angry. What she couldn't understand, though, was why such a slight to Josh should offend her so much.

CHAPTER NINETEEN

It was Josh's last night at Mrs. Brown's boardinghouse. He had given short notice, but she understood the circumstances for such a quick departure. He had already begun working for Miss Duffy and was getting to know the workers and learning how the entire house-building process could be managed. Luckily one of the laborers had recommended a man by the name of Rojas to help out. Josh had hired Rojas and was already reaping the benefits of the experience that the other man shared.

Josh was sitting on the sofa in the parlor of the boardinghouse alone. All of the ladies had been nice to spend their evening with him and they'd all said their farewells long ago before going up to their rooms for the night.

It was amazing how, in his ordinary day, he could function so well. But as soon as he was by himself, the hopelessness and sorrow over Gwen would wash over him. Between worrying over his new job and dreaming about Gwen, he wasn't sleeping well either. He decided to lie down on the sofa. Maybe a change of scenery would help him take a nap.

He was just about to doze off when he heard a creak on the stairs. He opened an eye and saw Bevin tiptoeing down. She was still wearing the peach-colored calico frock she'd had on earlier. He shut his eye when she started in his direction. He practically held his breath when she knelt down beside him.

"Are ye awake, Josh Flynn? I'd have a word with ye before ye go," she whispered in his ear.

He made a big show of waking, stretching, and acting pleasantly surprised as he sat up. "Hello there, Bevin. Have you something on your mind?"

"Aye." She settled next to him, arranging her skirts prettily. "I'm not one to mince words, mind," she stated.

"Go on," he encouraged.

"I think...I think you and I would be a good match. I thought I should say so before ye leave."

"Ah, well..." He tried to think of a gentle way to refuse her.

Her eyes held his as she said, "We've a common background. I'm loyal, and I find you're a fine cut of a man."

She seemed so sincere. It certainly was a balm to his wounded spirit. But, honestly, he knew he wasn't ready for this.

"Ah, Bevin..." he began.

She flung herself into his arms and squeezed him tightly. "We're both lonely, Josh."

He sighed and extricated himself. "'Tis sorry I am, Bevin, but my heart belongs to another...as I'm guessing yours does."

"You're wrong." Her eyes flashed. "Patrick is nothing to me."

"That still doesn't account for me," he explained.

Bevin sprang to her feet. "Is Gwen Sanders the reason for your melancholy? I saw you moonin' over her when she was here. Do I need to remind ye she's to be wed in a few months?" She was livid. Her normally pale complexion was bright red.

"Until she has a ring on her finger, I'll not give up," he retorted.

"You're a fool, Josh Flynn!" she said vehemently before turning her back on him and stomping up the stairs.

Josh arose. He knew all the commotion she was causing would likely rouse Mrs. Brown. He crept through the dark house as quickly as he could and went back to his place where he was safe, whether he could sleep or not.

The following morning, bleary-eyed as he was, Josh and the driver Miss Duffy had sent loaded his trunk and lumber into the back of a wagon. The driver waited in the seat while Josh went back to the carriage house one last time to see if he had forgotten anything. He found a rasp under a newspaper and picked it up.

As he emerged, Mac sauntered around the corner and mewed at him. Josh bent down and scratched behind the cat's scraggly ears. It was only the third time Josh had been allowed the honor to do so.

"Well, old man, I'm moving along. You can join me if you like." Josh grinned.

He started toward the front of the house, and about midway he noticed Mac was following him. As he prepared to climb aboard the wagon, he saw the cat was still there.

"Are you coming then?" He picked Mac up, expecting to get scratched or bitten. When that didn't occur, he placed him gently in the wagon bed. He assumed Mac would jump out, but when he didn't Josh took his own seat.

He tipped his cap to the driver and said, "I'm ready now."

~

Gwen, with notebook in hand, went up the wide limestone steps of the revival-style Carnegie Library at Oklahoma and Ash. She passed the enormous limestone columns and entered the tall doors. Gwen absolutely adored the tan brick-and-sandstone building that had been built in Guthrie several years earlier. Stepping onto the patterned tan tile in the central rotunda, she glanced up as she always did at the light streaming in from the domed ceiling. She liked the design of the building and how the central area led off to meeting and reading rooms under archways of carved molding atop large wooden columns.

After finding the nonfiction section, she perused the titles until she found some about Irish immigration. She carried them over to the long oak table in the general reading room and sat off by herself.

She opened the first book and read, taking notes as needed, for some time. It wasn't until she saw a moving etching of a family being separated as part of them boarded a ship for America that she realized she had done enough research and was ready to write. Imagining the setting in her mind's eye, she flipped to a blank page in her notebook. She tried to describe the scene in the opening paragraphs as vividly as possible but without unnecessary embellishments. The words kept flowing as she continued writing one scene to the next.

Time seemed to stand still for her until her stomach growled. Glancing around, she hoped no one else heard it. The clock on the wall showed it was one o'clock. Her mother would wonder why she hadn't returned for lunch. Picking up her things, she hurried out. Her heart pounded as quickly as her feet on the sidewalk. She was actually doing it. She was writing a novel.

Gwen spent her days composing her story and occasionally meeting Walter for lunch or supper. She was ready for a break when the Fourth of July rolled around. She spent the afternoon preparing and packing a large picnic basket with chicken sandwiches, coleslaw, potato salad, sweet and dill pickles, and apple pie.

Walter arrived promptly at six that evening. He helped her carry the assortment of baskets and quilts to his automobile. When all the items were aboard, Walter drove to Island Park south of town.

The park was already crowded when they pulled up. They walked to a shady spot under a large oak tree. They were close enough to the small island in Cottonwood Creek to see the wooden pavilion and hear the Capital City Band play.

They spread out the red-white-and-blue log cabin quilt and sat down to eat their supper. It was hot out, but the shade and a lazy breeze made their meal enjoyable.

Gwen swallowed a bite of potato salad before she commented, "I haven't told you yet, probably because I'm half afraid I will sabotage myself if I say it out loud, but…" Walter waited for her to continue.

"I've started writing a novel. I think it's going to be good." Gwen tried to restrain her enthusiasm.

He chewed thoughtfully, nodded, and finally said politely, "That's nice, Gwendolyn."

She wished to see some interest in his expression. She wanted to tell him all about her ideas and what she had accomplished so far. His reaction dampened her spirits considerably, but since she was not one to feel sorry for herself, she decided to ask him about his work.

"How are things at the office? You seem to be busy."

"Yes." He sat up straighter. "I currently have several extremely important cases."

"Really? Like what?"

"It's all confidential, of course," he said importantly.

"Oh yes, of course," she replied, half-embarrassed that she had asked.

They continued eating in silence. Neither of them was much for idle chitchat. After Walter finished his last swig of cider, he stood and breathed deeply.

"I believe I'll go stretch my legs. Would you like to join me?" he asked.

"I would, but I'm not quite done and I should put everything away."

"Yes. I'll go on and return shortly. We can then take a stroll together."

"That sounds nice," Gwen agreed.

He sauntered away. She watched him greeting people he knew until he disappeared from her line of sight.

"Hello there, Gwen." A female voice behind her startled her.

Gwen choked on the juice from the pickle she had been eating and coughed and coughed.

"Are you going to be all right?" Tina asked as she came into Gwen's line of sight and made herself comfortable on the quilt.

Gwen nodded and whispered hoarsely, "Yes." She spent several moments trying to clear her throat and regain her composure. She dabbed her eyes with a napkin. Of all people to practically choke to death in front of.

Tina's look of concern was quickly replaced by her normal merry expression. "Walter told me he was bringing you here tonight. Where is he?" she asked, looking around.

"He's here somewhere. He should return shortly if you need him for something," Gwen answered as she began to pack things away.

"Actually, I want to talk with *you*." Tina leaned forward as if she wanted to conspire with Gwen. "I was thinking we should have a surprise party for Walter's birthday next month."

"I don't know. Walter doesn't like surprises."

"Fiddlesticks! Who wouldn't want a party? He will be thirty, for goodness' sakes. We can't let that pass without a celebration."

"You're probably right."

"Oh, good." Tina clapped her hands. "I'll put together an invitation list of his associates and his more prestigious clientele. You can do the list for friends and your family. Do you want to have it at your house?"

"I'll have to see if it's fine with my mother."

Tina giggled. "Not your parents' house, silly goose, *your* house."

"Oh, yes. Certainly." Gwen wanted to blush. The house on Vilas Avenue had not even occurred to her.

"You will have to hurry and get that beautiful home furnished."

Gwen nodded, trying not to be daunted by the prospect of it.

"I'll contact caterers if you like," Tina offered.

Gwen raised her eyebrows.

"We can't have some of the most influential people in Guthrie eating our mamas' pies, can we?" Tina asked.

"I suppose not," Gwen assented.

"Good. I'm so excited!" Tina hopped up. She looked around and spotted Walter coming toward them. "There he is. I'll keep in touch." She winked at Gwen.

Walter strode up to them. Gwen stood and went to his side as he smiled and greeted Tina.

"I just stopped by to say hello," Tina said in her singsong way. "I'd better get back to my parents. They'll be wondering about me. I'll see you at the office tomorrow." She waggled her fingers at them and all but skipped away.

Gwen took Walter's arm and said, "I'm ready for that stroll now." She grinned up at him.

"Maybe later, Gwendolyn. I've warmed up." He unbuttoned his suit coat. "I believe I'd like to relax in the shade for now."

"That sounds good," she agreed, although she actually did wish to walk around. She put her wishes aside once again and settled down next to him to watch the entertainment, hear the speeches, and see the fireworks.

CHAPTER TWENTY

Josh was finally beginning to feel as though he was getting his feet under him. He had a good crew, and Rojas had recommended an excellent bricklayer and other tradesmen as needed. The house was coming along nicely. He also spent his spare time completing the dining room chairs and table. The table was definitely something he was proud of. It had a pedestal leg, two leaves, and the top was sturdy with no wobbles.

Josh showed it to Miss Duffy one day when she came by to check on things. She walked around the table and ran her fingers across it. She finally stopped and gave him an approving smile.

"Excellent, Mr. Flynn." Her tone was most sincere. "When my house is completed I will certainly promote you to all my acquaintances."

"I'd appreciate that, ma'am." He had been wondering something for some time and thought he might as well ask it. "So what made you take a chance on an inexperienced lad as myself for these jobs?"

She smiled wistfully. "Someone gave my da a chance when we moved to this country. He always tried to help people, and so have I."

He nodded. "Well, I want you to know I do realize what an opportunity this is, and I intend to make the best of it."

"I know you will," she said confidently. She studied his face a moment before concern shadowed her features. "Have you been sleeping well? Is there anything wrong with your accommodations?"

"No, no. Everything here is fine. It's one of the nicest bachelor flats I've had."

"Hmm." She didn't seem to believe him. "You don't appear to be as…rested…as you should be. Is the work too much?"

"No. I enjoy it." He tried to decide quickly how much he should say. "I've had some…personal problems…of late. Someone who meant a lot to me moved away. She didn't want to stay." He refrained from saying, "with me."

"Ah." She nodded her head solemnly. "A woman. I should have guessed." She patted his shoulder. "If it's meant to be, it will happen. Until then, don't make yourself sick over it. No woman is that important," she said wisely before she rustled away.

As he watched her walk toward her buggy, he sighed. He wished he could agree with her.

$\sim$

"It's so nice of you to shop for furniture with me, Walter," Gwen said, squeezing his arm as they entered an upscale store on Oklahoma Avenue. "This will be fun."

"Tina said this was the best shop in town. Let's see what they have." He glanced up at the second floor at the rear of the deep building. "I only have an hour free. We will need to hurry."

An earnest-looking young man with black hair and wire spectacles came up to them, introduced himself as Chad, and offered to show them around.

"Well, Chad, we need a house full of furniture and in not much time," Walter stated importantly.

Chad's eyes widened for a moment before he regained his composure. "Let's begin with the parlor then," he said as he led the way.

Walter stopped in front of a fully upholstered parlor suite with simple curved arms. Chad extolled the virtues of the hardwood bracing, the tempered steel springs, and the French tapestry.

"What's your opinion, Gwendolyn?" Walter asked as he pondered the sofa and three armchairs.

Honestly, she preferred the daintier styles with exposed carved wood, but Walter was a large man. He should probably have durable furniture. "I like it," she said.

"It comes in dark green or blue," Chad piped up.

Walter raised an eyebrow at Gwen in silent question.

"I like green," she commented.

"We'll have to order the green," Chad informed her.

"How long would that take?" Gwen asked.

"Two or three weeks."

That would be too close to Walter's birthday for comfort. "We should have the blue then," Gwen said.

Walter nodded. "We'll take it and a couple of those little tables too."

"Yes, sir," Chad's voice squeaked a tad. He cleared his throat. "The dining sets are just this way."

Walter was drawn right away to a massive quarter-sawn golden-oak table with huge swirled, carved legs resting on large balled feet. Once again, Gwen was pulled toward a darker, deeply carved walnut piece nearby.

"This one extends to twelve feet," Chad explained about the one Walter was looking at.

"We'll take it and twelve matching chairs."

"There is also a sideboard with a mirror that accompanies it," Chad suggested.

"Yes, of course. We'll have that as well," Walter agreed.

"Perfect, sir. This way to the bedroom suites."

Gwen tried not to feel embarrassed as she walked up the stairs with the men. Who would have guessed looking at beds would cause her to feel shy all of a sudden? She stood back as Walter approved another oak piece with at least a six-foot-tall rectangular headboard.

Walter gave her a look to see if she agreed. She could only nod her head as he informed Chad they would buy it and a matching dresser and washstand.

They followed Chad back downstairs so he could write up the order.

"Anything else?" Walter asked her.

She had her grandmother's rocking chair and a small writing desk in her room that she would be bringing with her. She shook her head. "I can't think of anything right away."

"Good. I'll go with him to set up an account," he informed her.

After Walter left, Gwen sank onto a nearby sofa. Her legs were weak and her head spun as she tried to figure how much money they had just spent. It had to be close to one hundred dollars and Walter hadn't even batted an eyelash. She was used to living frugally and paying cash for everything. She didn't like the thought of buying items on credit. It just seemed as if a person could get into a heap of trouble that way. It was certainly going to be different living in that manner.

$\sim$

The lock clicked as Gwen turned the key. She opened the door to the house on Vilas and stepped in to wait for the deliverymen. Her footsteps echoed on the oak floors of the empty house. She carried a notebook with her and went from room to room writing down things that were needed. Rugs, drapes, bookcases, and artwork were among the many items to purchase. Luckily the previous owner had left a large cupboard and icebox in the kitchen.

She would have to find stoneware for everyday use and china for special occasions. She had inherited some silverware from a great-aunt and had some linens she had collected over the years in her hope chest.

She went into the large dining room and stood in front of a row of windows looking out into the tiny backyard. The sun coming in the south windows made her uncomfortably warm. She moved away and sighed as she studied the empty room. It would barely be large enough for the huge set Walter had bought.

There was so much to do, and it made her weary just thinking about it all. She didn't understand why she wasn't more inspired about decorating her future home. It didn't make sense. She should be incredibly excited about her marriage and all that surrounded it. Especially since it was something she had anticipated for years. She had heard about people getting cold feet before their wedding. Maybe that's all this was. A little anxiety about spending the rest of your life with someone was surely normal.

By the time she had convinced herself she was sane after all, a loud rap came at the front door. She let the deliverymen in and tried to stay out of the way while directing their placement of furniture. She marveled at how quickly the job was completed.

She walked around after they left to make sure things were fine. The house didn't seem so empty and forlorn now. And even though there was still a lot of work to do, she wasn't quite as discouraged as before.

Gwen left the house, locking the door behind her, and walked to Madame Lorraine's. She had had her final fitting a few days previous and her wedding gown was finished. She entered the shop, paid the bill for the extra alterations, expressed her gratitude to Madame Lorraine for her artistry, and carried the muslin-covered dress home. She laughed at herself, knowing she must look quite a sight carrying the huge, fluffy bundle through the streets.

Finally she arrived home and struggled through the door, hoping her mother somehow wouldn't notice and ask to see the completed product. She hadn't told her mother about the changes she had requested and would just as soon put it off for another day.

Of course, luck wasn't in Gwen's favor. Her mother was sitting in the parlor, doing some embroidery. She arose and met her, closing the door behind them.

"Is this your wedding gown?" her mother asked, relieving Gwen of her burden and carrying it over to the sofa.

"Yes," Gwen answered.

"Let's see it," her mother said enthusiastically.

"We wouldn't want it to get dirty, would we?"

"Oh, for goodness' sakes, it's not as if George and Gilbert were going to handle it. I'll be ever so careful," she said playfully as she unwrapped the dress.

Her mother gaped at it. Her expression went from happiness to disdain. "There must be a mistake. This isn't your dress."

"Actually it is," Gwen said quietly.

"I don't understand. This isn't the design I showed to Madame Lorraine."

"I know." Gwen ducked her head apologetically. "I asked her to make the alterations. I paid for them myself."

There was no mistaking the disappointment in her mother's eyes. "It is not what Walter wanted."

"But it's what *I* want," Gwen said determinedly. It wasn't often she went against her mother's wishes.

Her mother stared at her for a moment before covering the gown up again. She turned her back on her, walked toward her chair, and said, "That's between the two of you then."

CHAPTER TWENTY-ONE

Gwen had never been so nervous. She told Walter she wanted to stop by their house before going to the restaurant for his birthday because she claimed she had a present stored there for him. Walter noted the abundance of buggies near their place as they drove down the street and she was afraid her ruse would be discovered.

"Someone must be having a party," he commented as the automobile came to a stop.

"You never know," she said lightheartedly. She quickly took off her traveling garb, stowed it in the seat, patted her upswept hair, and hoped she looked presentable in a new sky-blue taffeta gown edged with ecru lace.

They went up the walkway. Walter unlocked the door.

"It's right in here," Gwen said loudly.

At the cue, Tina turned on the electric lights and everyone shouted, "Surprise!"

Walter appeared dumbfounded for a moment, but as he recognized his friends, coworkers, and acquaintances a smile began to creep on his face.

He leaned down to Gwen's ear and asked, "Was this your idea?"

She wasn't sure if he was happy about the party or not. "Well, actually, it was Tina's idea. I told her you didn't like surprises," she whispered back.

"Well, it's fine. *This* time."

He kissed Gwen on the cheek, apparently to show his approval of the gathering. He removed his driving goggles, hat, and overcoat and handed them to Gwen. She went to put them away in one of the bedrooms as he began to mingle with the guests.

After she came back downstairs, she went straight for the kitchen to see about the hors d'oeuvres. Tina was about to exit with a tray of savory tea sandwiches.

"Wasn't he surprised?" Tina beamed.

"Yes, he was," Gwen agreed.

"I knew he would love it. This will be the most talked about soiree Guthrie has seen in a while," Tina said with triumphant satisfaction. "Judge Parker is even here. This is just fantastic!" Tina left all aglow and extremely happy with herself.

Gwen's mother seemed pleased also as she busied herself with a plate of cheese and crackers. She was always comfortable in social situations.

"I agree. This is quite a function, Gwen. You've done well." She picked up the dish and paused. "Don't forget. I'll have to leave earlier than the other guests to check on the boys."

"Yes, of course." Gwen nodded.

Her brothers hadn't been invited to the adult gathering. Gilbert had protested about being left out, but George seemed content to stay at home.

"I'll take these out." Her mother motioned to her full hands. "And I *must* go talk with Mrs. Winston. I haven't seen her in ages." Her mother was an ageless, confident beauty as she mixed with everyone.

Gwen sighed and wished she felt as carefree as the others seemed to be. She was always nervous when she went to these kinds of functions with Walter, and tonight she was supposed to be the hostess. She hoped it all went well. She picked up a platter of little tea cakes and cookies to take to the refreshment table in the parlor.

As she made her way through the crowded room, she saw her mother conversing with Mrs. Winston, and she saw Walter and Tina talking to an extremely well-dressed matronly lady. She spoke rather thunderously and Gwen overheard her easily.

"And just think, Mr. Manning, after seeing the two of you so many times in the café, how astonished I was to learn that Miss Randolph was your employee! I was mighty amazed to see you enter with that *other* young lady!" She laughed boisterously at herself.

Walter and Tina exchanged glances. Walter smiled as Tina giggled.

"Miss Randolph and I work over lunch at times when we are busy," he explained.

Gwen didn't have time to ponder that exchange as a young woman shyly asked her where the necessary room was. After she pointed it out, an associate of Walter's, Mr. Bryant, asked if there was any beverage stronger than punch available. She hurried to the kitchen and returned with a bottle of red wine and some glasses.

Mr. Bryant was at her side as soon as she began to pour the burgundy liquid. He took a full glass from her, breathed in the scent, and exhaled blissfully. "Extraordinary. Imagine, if the tee-totalers get their way, Oklahoma will be a dry state." He shook his head and took a sip. "It's a shame, I say," he muttered as he walked away.

Gwen chuckled to herself as she poured a few more glasses and then picked one up to take to Walter. He was visiting with a couple of important-looking gentlemen, so she paused nearby, not wanting to interrupt. Two people tried to pass by her at the same time. They each inadvertently nudged her and she accidentally tipped her glass. She was horrified to see red wine splash all over the front of her skirt.

She caught Walter's eye as she began to rush away and saw a flicker of disappointment from him before he returned to his conversation. Her cheeks burned the color of the stain on her gown as she all but ran to the sanctuary of the kitchen. She put the empty glass down, found a rag, dampened it, and scrubbed at her skirt, knowing the spots wouldn't come out.

Tears welled in her eyes. If only Ada were here. She would tell her she could repair the damage with a bit of lace here or material there. Or if Rose were here, she would reassure her that it wasn't the end of the world and that accidents like this happen to everyone. But her best friends in the world weren't here. Instead, she was little more than hired help to a bunch of people she barely knew and some she didn't even care for.

Her heart grew heavy as she realized how much she didn't want to be here. She wiped tears that threatened to fall. Digging around in a drawer, she found a crisp new apron that she had unpacked the day before. She put it on to cover the stain and took a deep, shaky breath before rejoining the party.

She stood in the doorway to the parlor and searched for Walter. He was standing next to Mr. Bryant and Tina. Tina was chattering away as usual. Mr. Bryant and Walter laughed at something she said. The sight took Gwen aback. Walter actually laughed out loud. Gwen couldn't remember if she had ever heard him do such a thing. He was never, ever that jovial around her. And the wonder of it all was that she wasn't in the least bit jealous or upset about it.

It was at that moment that she finally, after all those wasted years, realized she did not love Walter. She could barely say she was even fond of him. All of a sudden, she was exhausted and she was tired of pretending. She wanted to tell Walter their relationship was over so she didn't have to continue the charade any longer. Most of all, she wanted this ridiculous party to end. She wanted to be rid of Walter and his pompous behavior and his equally absurd friends once and for all.

Ending her engagement would cause a terrible fuss. Walter would not like to hear their marriage was off. Her mother would be furious. But how could Gwen marry a man she didn't love? She suddenly remembered Rose's comment, *Which is more honorable? To marry someone you love or someone you don't?* At the time, Gwen had thought it meant she should marry Walter, but as she analyzed the words she knew it could also be taken the other way.

Had her friends known all along that she didn't love Walter enough to marry him? She wondered why they had never said anything about it. But she also realized that, with her stubborn personality, she probably wouldn't have listened to them anyway.

She knew it would not be easy to tell Walter she wanted to break off their engagement, but she knew she could do it. And no amount of scandal would stop her now.

~

Gwen couldn't, in good conscience, leave the house a shambles, so after the last guest left she cleaned everything while Walter sat on the new sofa in the parlor. It was a tad disconcerting as he watched her move about the place. She felt as if she was being scrutinized, and she did not like it.

After she put the final dish away, she gathered the few personal linens she had brought with her. Luckily she hadn't moved in any of her other things yet, and she didn't care for anything else in the house. She dropped her bundle by the front door with Walter's driving clothes that she had brought down earlier.

She braced herself for the conversation ahead. Gwen knew what she had to do, but it still didn't make the process any easier. Her heart was pounding and her hands were sweaty. She went to Walter and stopped before him. He glanced up at her.

"Walter, I don't think we should get married," she said bluntly.

"Don't be ridiculous," he said placidly.

"I'm serious." She stood her ground.

He arose slowly and deliberately. He held her gaze determinedly. "Our wedding is in three months. We are not going to cancel it."

"We have to…I don't think we love each other as an engaged couple should."

"Is that what this is about? Of course I love you."

"Then kiss me and prove it," she dared him. She held her face up toward his. Maybe, just maybe, if she could feel any sort of passion from him, he might change her mind.

He crossed his arms and said in a tone that assured her his patience was running thin, "I won't play some senseless game. I said I love you."

She searched his eyes for any sign of affection and saw none. "I'm sorry, Walter. This won't work."

"You don't love me. That's it, isn't it?" His voice began to increase in volume. "You want that Irishman, don't you? You're leaving me for an Irish railroad worker!"

"No! Josh has nothing to do with this."

"His name was Flynn, wasn't it?" He ignored her statement. "Gwen Flynn. How quaint." He snorted.

"We are *friends*. That's all," she said angrily.

"As if anyone would believe that. Tina was right. Any woman who loved her man wouldn't stay away from him unless there was someone else keeping her away."

"So Tina is the one who put that notion in your head? I thought so."

"Tina is the epitome of a lady," he said defensively.

"Oh, please. She wouldn't be gallivanting all around town with an engaged man if she cared about being a proper lady."

"Are you insinuating that Tina and I—" His face reddened with fury.

"No. I'm not. I'm only friends with Josh. At this point, I'm sure you're only friends with Tina. You're not stupid. You wouldn't damage your career like that."

"You're right. I wouldn't," he said vehemently. "And how do you think a broken engagement will affect my career?"

"Wouldn't a divorce be more scandalous?" she asked brusquely.

He seemed appalled that she would even utter the word. They stood facing each other for the longest time.

"I had a feeling I shouldn't have started courting you," he stated with contempt.

She knew it was an insult but chose to ignore it. "I want a happy marriage. I want you to have one also. I'm not myself when I'm with you. We would only be miserable."

He continued to stare at her for what seemed like minutes. Finally he asked, "Is that all you have to say about the matter?"

"Yes," she said simply.

"If we leave this room with this done, I will *not* take you back. Do you understand? If we break off this engagement tonight, it will be forever," he said haughtily.

"I understand."

He shook his head in disgust. "Let's go. I'm finished talking about this."

Striding past her, he went out the door, and was waiting in the automobile before she could collect her things. He was stony as he drove. When he stopped in front of her parents' house, he continued to look straight ahead with his hands gripping the steering wheel.

Gwen opened her own door and held her things to her chest as she watched him. "I'm sorry," she offered.

"You should be," he said spitefully before putting the vehicle in gear and driving off.

Gwen let out a long, loud sigh. She was so glad that was over with. Walter was angry with her now, but she knew Tina would be right there to console him. She would soon be a distant memory to Walter.

She had one more difficult task to accomplish. She had to tell her mother, and she knew that wouldn't go well.

A parlor light was still on even though she knew her brothers were long in their beds. She crept in quietly, hoping against hope that her mother was also asleep. She thought she was going to escape a confrontation with her mother until she saw her coming down the stairs in her nightclothes with an oil lamp.

"You needn't have stayed up, Mama," Gwen commented quietly.

"I always want to be assured of your safety," she whispered. Her eyes twinkled in the lamplight. "And tonight I wanted to see how things went after I left."

Gwen shifted uneasily from foot to foot. "The guests seemed to have a good time...but..."

"But what?" she asked.

"Well...after everyone left..." She paused. There was no easy way to say it. "Walter and I decided not to get married," she blurted.

Her mother chuckled lightly. "No need to worry, dear. Walter will be back tomorrow and all will be well." She smiled. "I don't know how many times your father and I called our wedding off, but we reconciled every time."

"No. There won't be reconciliation," Gwen said adamantly.

"Why?" her mother asked suspiciously.

"Because I told him I didn't think we loved each other enough."

"For heaven's sake, Gwen!" her mother whispered fiercely. "Life is not like those silly novels you read and write. Sometimes one must put aside childish fantasies and do what's best for them. Walter has promise, a future. You would live in comfort for the rest of your life."

"What good is security if you're bound to someone who makes you as miserable as you make them?" she asked defiantly.

"You will apologize to Walter tomorrow. After all I've done to endear you to him, I won't accept this. I won't let you disgrace us or him."

Gwen exhaled slowly, trying not to get angry. "I will not beg him to take me back. I do not want Walter. I will *not* marry him," she said forcefully as she hurried up to her bedroom, leaving her stunned mother at the foot of the stairs.

CHAPTER TWENTY-TWO

Gwen's mother remained angry and would not speak with her for several days. When Gwen's father came home and heard the news, he was none too pleased, but he finally reassured her. He told her that if she truly felt she was doing the right thing, everything would work out in the end. Her brothers were more upset about losing the privilege of an occasional ride in an automobile than by the loss of Walter himself.

So to get her mind off her domestic troubles, Gwen continued to write. She spent every moment she could scribbling away. As her hand glided across the pages and her mind focused on the people in this other world, she began to feel free. She was free to create and free from the burden of marrying a man she didn't love. She would never tell her mother, but it was the most content she had been in years.

~

One Sunday after church in the middle of August, Josh visited with Luke and Ada. Little Lucy could hold herself erect by now and had big, inquisitive eyes. It was difficult to tell yet whether she was going to have green or brown eyes, but it was already certain she would be as pretty as her mother.

"We're going to Guthrie in a few days," Luke said. "I was wonderin' if you might be able to stay out at the place overnight and take care of the animals for me? I didn't know if you'd be able to get off at the building site for that long or not."

"What days would it be?" Josh asked.

"We'd leave on Friday and be back Saturday night."

"I don't know why I couldn't, but I'll check with Miss Duffy."

"Good." Luke nodded. "But if it'll be a problem, I could probably get the Engels to come by and check on things. Just telephone and let me know."

Lucy stretched out a tiny hand and seemed to reach for Josh. Ada gave the baby to him. Lucy was still a tiny thing. Since he was used to carrying around lumber all day long, it seemed as if she hardly weighed anything. It was soon apparent that he wasn't the reason for her interest; his red neck scarf was. Her soft fingers touched his neck as she tried to get a mouthful of the material.

"Now, Lucy, don't ruin Josh's nice clothes," Ada said in a motherly tone as she tried to pry the silk out of the baby's fingers.

"It's all right." Josh chuckled and shifted Lucy so she couldn't reach it. She focused on her fingers instead.

"We're going to Guthrie to celebrate Luke's birthday with his family and to let them see Lucy," Ada told him.

"Aye?" Josh raised an eyebrow.

"Yes." Ada nodded. "We'll be seeing Gwen and her family too."

"Hmm." He didn't like how his heart flip-flopped at the mere mention of her name.

"Is there anything you'd like us to tell her?" Ada asked.

Josh shook his head. "Just tell her...I said hello."

~

Gwen was in a madhouse. Her uncle Leo and aunt Faye's house, to be exact. They were having a family reunion and birthday celebration for Luke. He was there with Ada and Lucy. Luke's older brothers, Peter, Mark, and John, were present with their wives and children of all ages. Plus her family made quite a crowd in her uncle's modest two-story home.

It was late in the afternoon when Gwen finally found a quiet spot in the rear yard to visit with Ada and Luke. She sat on a bench with Ada and Lucy while Luke lounged against a young pecan tree.

"So where's Manning?" Luke asked as he put a blade of grass in his mouth.

"Oh, well...I haven't told the two of you yet...it just didn't seem appropriate to tell in a letter or over the telephone..." Gwen struggled.

Ada and Luke were rapt with attention.

"Did somethin' happen?" Luke scowled.

"I broke off my engagement with Walter."

"What?!" Luke exclaimed as he sat up straighter.

Ada was surprisingly silent.

Gwen stroked little Lucy's head. "I told him I didn't want to marry him."

"Are you sure?" Ada asked.

"Yes," Gwen replied confidently.

There was a long pause while they considered her announcement. They finally both grinned from ear to ear.

"Good," Luke announced. "I never cared for the fella."

It was Gwen's turn to be astounded. "You didn't?" She glared at her cousin. "Why in the world didn't you tell me?"

He chuckled. "Would it have made any difference? Besides, who was I to stand between you, love, and Aunt Grace?"

Gwen sighed. "I guess you're right, but I still wish someone would have said something."

"Rose and I wanted to. We even attempted to say something once..." Ada began, "but you always seemed so adamant about your affections toward Walter that we didn't exactly feel we should try to deter you."

Gwen nodded. "You're right. I probably wouldn't have listened."

Luke took his watch out of his vest pocket, opened the cover, and observed the time. He stood and brushed grass off his trousers.

"It's time to head for the station. We don't want to miss the train. Flynn will be waitin' for us in Shawnee with our wagon." Luke held out a hand to Ada to help her up.

"It's time already?" Ada asked. "I've barely been able to chat with Gwen."

"Sorry about that, but by the time we say good-bye to everyone, we'll have to hurry."

They started toward the house.

"So why would Josh have your wagon?" Gwen wondered out loud.

"He's watchin' the place while we're gone," Luke answered.

"The railroad let him off?"

"He doesn't work there anymore," Ada said. "He's helping Miss Duffy, the one he was making the furniture for, build her new home."

"That's interesting."

Luke stopped in his tracks and snapped his fingers. "Now that's a man you should be lookin' at, Gwen. He seems like an all-around good fella."

"We're just friends," she protested automatically.

"He's worth takin' a look at anyway. Think about it," he instructed.

"Yes, sir," Gwen joked.

"Good." Luke grinned before opening the back door.

"Oh, and speaking of Josh…can you not tell him about Walter and me? I'd like to speak to him in person…someday…soon," Gwen said.

Luke nodded thoughtfully. "If you don't take too long about it. There's no use in a man pinin' away for a woman that's free for the askin'."

"He misses me?" Gwen asked. Her pulse quickened just thinking about it.

"He does look a little tired and thin," Ada commented.

"I'm sorry for that, but I'm not ready…" She paused. "Please don't tell him about my breaking off the engagement," Gwen begged. "I'll talk to him soon. I promise."

Luke gave her a peck on the cheek. "I'll keep quiet."

"Thank you."

Gwen hugged and kissed them and watched as they said their farewells to the rest of the family. Uncle Leo drove off with them and she couldn't help wishing she was going back to Shawnee, but she was a tad frightened about who and what awaited her there. She definitely wasn't ready to think about all that.

So instead of pondering Josh, Gwen spent several days completing her book. The day she wrote the final word was a glorious day indeed. She reread and edited it as she went along. She was amazed that she had actually finished the project. She didn't know if she would ever attempt to get it published, but it was deeply satisfying knowing that she had done something she always wanted to do.

She stacked the papers into a neat pile, unrolled a long length of wide red ribbon, and tied the pages together with a big bow on top. She laid it gently in her desk drawer for safekeeping.

As she glanced up, she saw a male figure on the walkway below. Her heart actually skipped a beat before she realized it was only George. For a second she had thought it was Josh.

She picked up the small cross that was sitting on the windowsill that Josh had made for her. She touched the intricately carved treasure and she could almost feel the love that had gone into it.

Heaving a terrible sigh, she plopped onto the red-and-white quilt on her bed. She couldn't put it off any longer. She had to wrestle with the lion that had been glaring at her for some time. Josh would laugh if he knew she thought of him in that way. But it was the truth. She was terrified of him and all the emotions concerning him.

She stared at the red roses on the wallpaper. It had been years since she had given up her childhood fantasy of Josh returning and declaring his love. When he had finally found her and told her all the things she had longed to hear, she had thought it was too late. What was she to do now that she was free? Did they really know each other well enough as adults to profess their undying love? She wasn't sure.

So she ticked off the things she knew about him now. He was funny. She had always liked that about him. He was sincere. That was a trait she admired in any person. He was a talented woodworker. Creative people inspired her. And he was definitely handsome. A slow grin spread across her face. Previously, she had been so focused on *not* noticing his physical attributes when they were together, but she found herself extremely happy to think about them now. His jet hair, dark eyes, and lean physique were very appealing to her. She blushed as she thought of his lips and how it felt when he kissed her. She had been appalled at the time, but now she wished for more.

That settled it. She was sure she loved Josh. She couldn't help it. She always had. Now what to do about it?

Rolling off the bed, she went to her desk. She found a fresh sheet of stationery and sat down. Knowing she always expressed herself better in writing, she opened the ink bottle and dipped her pen. She wrote:

> *Dearest Josh,*
> *You were right. I'm sure you know how much it costs for me to admit it.*

I canceled my wedding to Walter. It was difficult, but I know it was for the best. I thought my honor would be intact by staying with him, but what good is my appearance to everyone else when that marriage would have been a fraud?

I must tell you how dear you have always been to me. I tried to forget you. I could not.

If I run back to you, will you accept me? Will you hold me and make the promises I've longed to hear?

Please let me know and I will leave this life behind.

Gwen

Gwen blew on the ink to ensure it was dry. Folding the letter, she inserted it into an envelope, addressed it in care of Mrs. Brown's boardinghouse, and put a stamp on it. She would carry the letter to the post office herself; she didn't want this one to get waylaid. She hurried out of her room, down the stairs, and began walking toward the post office before she completely lost her nerve.

CHAPTER TWENTY-THREE

Gwen waited and waited for word from Josh. She wasn't a patient person by nature and the experience was difficult for her. In the meantime, she made peace with her parents. They came to an acceptance of sorts regarding the situation, even though they still were not fond of her decision.

She also tried to find things to occupy her mind and hands. She wasn't a proficient seamstress by anyone's standards, so she tried to improve her skill by embroidering Celtic designs on doilies and towels. Her efforts were filled with an abundance of knots and loose threads, but she felt she was making some headway.

When mid-September rolled around without any response from Josh, she tried not to be dismayed. The date of his birthday was quickly approaching and she assumed he would contact her before then. She almost thought about going to Shawnee, casually, of course, to see him and give him birthday wishes in person, but she decided against it.

She was afraid he was angry with her and didn't want to talk to her. Another fear was that he would never forgive her. Worst of all, she was anxious about the thought that he was courting someone like Bevin. For her own sanity, she tried not to dwell on that possibility.

~

Josh had to admit he was proud of himself. The exterior of Miss Duffy's house was done and he and the crew had moved inside for the finishing work. He had personally worked on the dining room. He had arranged for someone to wallpaper the room with the rich plum-and-green-striped paper Miss Duffy had picked out, while he hand-carved grapes and vines on the crown molding. After the wallpaper was up, he installed the molding and the paneled wainscoting. When everything was completed, he asked Rojas to help him move in the table and chairs.

He tried not to express too much self-satisfaction as he showed the room to Miss Duffy. He was touched by her enthusiasm as she dabbed tears with a lacy handkerchief.

"It surpasses my imagination, Mr. Flynn," Miss Duffy said as she put her shoulders back and collected herself. "I've been considering a proposition for quite a while and I'd like to talk to you about it now."

"Aye?"

"I'd like to be your benefactor. After you've finished my home, I would like you to live in the carriage house free of charge, and you've only to keep an eye on things for me. That should allow you the freedom to make your art without any financial worries." Her gaze was steady and determined. "I've also thought about the fact that you may want to marry and start a family one day. I would be willing, if your future wife agrees, for you and your family to continue to live here. We could add on to the carriage house or you could live in the third story."

To say Josh was speechless was an understatement. He opened his mouth once but couldn't speak. Finally he swallowed and said, "I'm overwhelmed, Miss Duffy. Why in the world would you want to do something so generous? I mean, how does the situation benefit you?"

Miss Duffy smiled. She did not seem taken aback by the question. "I'm an old woman. I have no children. I've no family left. This house was to be a sort of legacy so I could feel I made some sort of impression in this world. But I've come to realize that it's the people that matter. I can make a difference for better or worse in someone's life. And maybe one day I'll have at least one person mourn my passing."

Josh appreciated her heartfelt answer. He wouldn't have stood for charity. He extended his hand. "I accept," he said as he shook her hand. "And ye can rest knowin' ye'll have the grandest wake in the territory."

Miss Duffy chuckled. "Good. That's all I ask."

She turned to leave, then paused. "By the way, have you heard from your young lady that moved away?"

Josh cleared his throat, feeling a tad self-conscious. "No...and I'm beginning to think I won't."

"'Tis a shame," she commented as she walked ahead of him. "But if she can't see what a fine young man you are, it's her loss."

Josh wanted to agree, but truthfully he felt he was the one who was defeated. If he hadn't had such interesting work to do, he would hate to think what would have become of him.

~

As the days began to cool and September slid into October, Gwen could stand the suspense no longer. She had to find out if Josh was alive or dead or seeing another woman. Whatever his fate, she needed to know.

So on one brisk, clear autumn afternoon she decided to telephone Ada. Her mother customarily took a cup of tea out to the large rear porch to enjoy a tranquil moment before the boys returned from school. Gwen waited until her mother was settled at the black wrought-iron chair and table before poking her head out the back screen door.

"I'm going to call Ada and Luke. I haven't talked to them in a while," Gwen announced.

Her mother blew on her tea and took a sip before she said, "That sounds good, dear. Tell them to give the baby a kiss for me."

Gwen closed the screen door, wishing she could shut the solid wood door also to block her end of the conversation, but knew her mother would be automatically suspicious if she did so.

She went to the oak telephone on the wall in a corner by the back door. Her mother had not been thrilled about having the modern convenience mingle with her decor, so she had it installed as out of sight as possible.

Gwen talked to the operator and the telephone was soon ringing on the other end.

"Hello?" Ada's voice asked.

"Hi there. How is everyone?" Gwen asked, hoping she was speaking loud enough for Ada to hear, but not her mother.

"We're good. Lucy is growing. How are you?"

"I'm fine." She paused. "I was wondering about Josh. How is he?"

"Have you talked to him yet?" Ada asked.

"I sent him a letter explaining things…but I haven't heard from him."

"We were wondering if he knew. The last time I saw him at church, he looked as if he was wasting away. It appears as if he hasn't eaten or slept well in months." Ada's voice was concerned.

"Truthfully?"

"Yes. Luke really wants to talk to Josh, but I've made him wait. I'm not sure how much longer he'll hold off, though. We're both a little worried about him."

"I don't know what to do," Gwen confessed. "Maybe he received my letter but is really angry or upset with me."

"I would write him another letter. There is the chance he didn't get the first one. If you don't get a response, I would come down here and see him yourself. Something isn't right."

"Yes," Gwen agreed. "Yes. I'll do that. I'll let you go for now. I'll talk to you again soon."

"Good-bye, Gwen."

Gwen hung the earpiece on the hook and was about to sneak upstairs when she heard her mother calmly call for her.

"Yes, Mama?" Gwen asked as she went out to the white porch.

"Sit down, please," her mother instructed as she motioned to another chair.

Gwen did as she was told and sat nervously while she waited for her mother to say something. She instinctively dreaded the conversation they were about to have.

"Did I hear you say you wrote a letter to Joshua Flynn?"

"Yes."

"Why would you do that?" her mother asked.

"He's a friend, and I thought he should know Walter and I are not getting married," Gwen answered.

"There was no ulterior motive?"

Gwen swore her mother must be able to read her mind sometimes. She didn't know how she did it. She might as well confess and get it over with. "I care for Josh. I wanted him to know."

"You didn't say anything scandalous in your letter, did you?"

"Of course not."

Her mother sighed. "You know I feel that he doesn't have good prospects."

"That shouldn't matter," Gwen said heatedly.

"But it does, Gwendolyn. A man needs to be able to take care of his family."

"Josh is a builder. He could make a house out of nothing. He's also an artist. It's amazing what he can do with wood. He's so talented, in fact, that a Miss Duffy has hired him to build a house for her," Gwen said defensively.

"Miss Duffy?" Her mother suddenly seemed interested. "Miss Cordelia Duffy from Shawnee?"

"I think so," Gwen responded.

"Cordelia Duffy is the most affluent woman in the territory. She recently spoke to our women's group at the library about philanthropy in all aspects of our lives and how to do so in a practical sense." Her mother paused to consider the matter. "If Josh Flynn is working for her and he does a good job, he is sure to have a promising future. She will see to that."

Gwen truthfully did not care if Josh ever made his fortune. She wanted the man, not a position in life. She waited for her mother to continue and watched her skeptically.

"In spite of what you might think, Gwen, I'm not an entirely contemptuous person. I do believe in giving people a chance to prove themselves." She leaned forward, took Gwen's hand, and squeezed it. Her eyes were sincere and touched with sadness. "You are my only daughter. I know you're a woman now, but I still want to look out for you."

Gwen nodded, knowing her mother's words were heartfelt.

"If you continue to write to Josh, will you let your father and I have a long talk with him? We want to be assured he's good enough for you before any courting goes on."

"Oh, Mama. I don't even know if he will write me back. I've no idea if he even still has feelings for me. But I do promise to not keep my actions secret."

"I would appreciate that, dear." Her mother smiled.

They heard the front door slam and boots galloping through the house. The boys were home.

Her mother rose. "I'd better get them a snack before they tear up my kitchen."

Gwen decided to stay outside in the solitude. She was glad she had talked with her mother after all. She didn't feel they were total opposites anymore, and for that she was grateful.

Now all that remained was to write another letter to Josh and see if he would respond. She wasn't sure what she would do if he did not.

CHAPTER TWENTY-FOUR

Gwen didn't hear from Josh. To bide her time, she began to volunteer with her mother at an orphanage. She loved reading to the hopeful faces after her mother helped them with their music lessons. They both benefited tremendously from being with children who needed the acceptance and attention of adults.

As the days passed into November, Gwen found herself caught up in the excitement of pending statehood. It seemed the town of Guthrie and everyone in the twin territories waited for daily reports to see when President Roosevelt would sign the documents proclaiming Oklahoma a state. Gwen made it a habit to be the first one in the house to read the newspaper every day so she would know as soon as possible.

All sorts of festivities were planned. Parades, food, speeches, and an inaugural ball were being arranged. Gwen helped decorate the Carnegie Library with bunting and tried to assist in any way she could around town. It was a relief for her to think about something bigger than herself. She was thrilled to be in the center of history in the making.

~

One evening in the middle of the month in which Gwen was supposed to get married, Josh stood in the front yard of Miss Duffy's place after Rojas and the others had gone for the day. A fringe-topped surrey with a man and woman drove up the street. He watched as it stopped near him. The young man hopped down and assisted the young woman to the ground. He was truly surprised when Bevin walked toward him alone in what appeared to be a new royal-blue suit.

"Hello there, Bevin," he said warily. "What brings you out this way?"

She appeared somewhat nervous. "I've a confession to make."

"Shouldn't you talk to a priest about that?" he jested.

She smiled at him sheepishly. "I did that, but I still have to talk with you."

He raised his eyebrows, wondering what she was doing here.

"'Tis ashamed I am to admit it, but I was mad at you after you left and I was being spiteful and I can't believe meself that I did it, but after Patrick came to get me I remembered what I'd done and—"

"What are you blatherin' about, lass?" he interrupted. He had a feeling he wasn't going to like what she had to say.

She clamped her lips shut and pulled two envelopes out of her jacket pocket. "You received two letters after you left. I told Mrs. Brown I would bring them to you, but I didn't. I stowed them away. I didn't read them, mind you," she explained.

He took them from her and noted Gwen's name on the return address. He was angry, disgusted, and anxious.

"Go," he stated simply. "Go and never speak to me again." He glanced up long enough to see her pick up her skirts and dart off like a frightened rabbit.

"There's no need to fret about that, Josh Flynn," Bevin called over her shoulder. "Patrick and I were married today. I'm moving back home."

Josh didn't even wait for them to leave before he ran to the carriage house. He looked at the cancellation dates on the envelopes and ripped open the oldest letter. His hands shook as he read. Could it be true? Did he dare hope? He tore into the other letter. He scanned it. The words were almost identical.

It had been so long since she had sent them. Did she still feel the same or had she moved on? He silently cursed Bevin. If that spiteful girl had caused permanent damage by keeping these letters secret, he'd never forgive her.

That aside, what mattered was Gwen was not going to marry that Manning fellow. Most important was that Gwen cared for him. He wouldn't waste another moment. He climbed the stairs two at a time so he could pack.

As he was throwing clothes into his bag, he realized it would be too late to call on her tonight, and he would need to let Miss Duffy know his plans. But at dawn he would be on the first train to Guthrie.

~

The train was packed. Josh had never seen so many people crammed into a railroad car. Once he left Oklahoma City, he had to stand with other men.

By overhearing different conversations, he was able to gather that newspapers had reported the day before that President Roosevelt was going to sign documents that morning making Oklahoma a state. Folks were headed to the territorial capital to celebrate.

Inadvertently he was traveling to the busiest city in the new state to try to find Gwen. He'd left Shawnee without getting her parents' address from Luke or bringing her letters with him. Ah well, if that was the only foolish thing he did that day, he'd be all right.

~

Gwen was waiting with the crowd that surrounded the huge newspaper building on the corner of Second Street and Harrison Avenue. A telegram was supposed to arrive as soon as the president had signed the proclamation. Gwen was absolutely beside herself with anticipation. She tried to explain the significance of becoming the forty-sixth state to her brothers, but they were having more fun watching the boisterous people than trying to take in the historical event.

The morning was bright and chilly, but she was warm enough in a new brown serge flounced walking skirt and matching double-breasted fitted jacket with black piping. She had even stuck a black ostrich plume in her Sunday hat for the occasion. She wished Owen was here with his camera to record the day for posterity. Actually, she wished all her friends were here, especially Josh. It would have been all the more memorable.

Someone opened the door to the newspaper building. A man in a black suit came out with a pistol. He held it straight up and high over his head. The crowd hushed.

"Oklahoma is now a state!" he announced before shooting the gun in the air.

The throng erupted in cheers while the nearby militia returned the volley. A band started to play as Gwen squeezed her brothers affectionately. Through the cacophony, Gwen swore she heard someone call her name. She looked around, but didn't see anyone. She thought she must be mistaken.

"Gwen!" someone shouted from her right side.

She turned and saw Josh trying to elbow his way through the crazed throng. He was wearing a black suit and felt hat. He was smiling, but he looked tired, and his lean frame seemed thinner. Her heart almost hurt at the sight of him.

"Josh!" she exclaimed as he neared.

She threw herself into his arms and gave him a huge hug before she realized she didn't know the reason for his visit. He could be here to tell her he was getting married to Bevin for all she knew. Removing herself from his warm embrace, she glanced up at him self-consciously. She was glad her cheeks were already pink from the crisp air or he would see her blushing.

"Josh. It's so good to see you. What brings you here?" she asked as blithely as possible.

He appeared to be happy and sad at the same time. "Your letters," he answered seriously. He placed his hands on her upper arms and pulled her close so she could hear. "I moved when I started working for Miss Duffy. Bevin intercepted your letters and just yesterday felt guilty enough to bring them to me."

"So you and Bevin—"

"There never was me and Bevin. She tried to get my attention, but she wasn't you," he assured her.

Her emotions soared with every word. Were her hopes actually coming true? "When I didn't hear from you, I assumed—"

"I know. I felt the same." He caught her eyes with his and all the other people disappeared. "Could we begin again?" he asked. "As if none of that other business ever happened?"

"If you can forgive me for leaving."

"Aye." He touched her cheek gently. "I didn't like it, but I finally understood."

"Gwen?" George asked from behind her, tugging her sleeve.

"Who's this?" Gilbert asked bluntly as they both glared at Josh suspiciously.

Gwen laughed and stepped away from Josh, but kept her gloved hand on his forearm. She didn't want to be separated from him again. "This is an old *friend*," she explained with a grin aimed at Josh. "I knew him when you two were small."

She made introductions all around. Her brothers acted grown-up and protective of her. She thought it was sweet.

"Don't you believe we should take him home to Mother and Father?" George asked importantly.

"Aye. You're right, young man," Josh agreed. "I do need to speak with your parents."

Gwen cringed inwardly at the thought, but she had learned from experience that it was better to get the difficult things in life over with.

"Let's go then," she said. "We'll need to hurry. I don't want to miss the inauguration at the library."

They debated whether to catch a trolley and ride part of the way, but the streets were so congested and the trolleys so crowded that they estimated they could walk faster. They took off at a brisk pace, and before long the boys raced ahead. Josh and Gwen slowed so they could talk.

"I can't believe you're actually here," Gwen commented as she glanced sideways at him.

"I had to come." He paused, looking at her thoughtfully. "I promised you a long time ago that we'd be together again."

"I know, but we were so young."

"I never forgot you, Gwen. I may have courted a lass or two, but you were always with me." He placed a hand over his heart before continuing. "When I was in that train wreck last year...I knew I had to find you somehow. When I did, I knew it was meant to be."

"Even though Walter was in the picture?"

He nodded. "I felt so, but I also didn't think I should say anything...at first. The more time I spent with you, the more I realized you surpassed anything I'd ever imagined. There was no way I could stop myself from telling you how I felt."

"And I threw it in your face and ran away." She sighed. "That's why I'm surprised you came...I didn't know if you would still want—"

"After learning you were free, Gwen, I took the first train here. That should tell you how much I still want you."

Gwen was a bit overwhelmed by his forthrightness. Walter would never have done something so spontaneous or shared his feelings in such a way. It was exhilarating and frightening all at once. She knew her life was about to change. And truthfully, she couldn't wait.

Gilbert jogged back to them and said, "Come on, slowpokes. We're almost there."

Gwen walked with Josh the remaining distance in silence. There were so many questions she wanted to ask and things she wanted to say that she didn't know where to begin. As they went up the steps to her house, she realized that would all have to wait.

The boys had already run in and announced statehood and Josh's arrival, so by the time Gwen and Josh entered, her parents were waiting for them in the parlor. Her brothers had disappeared into the kitchen for a snack.

Her parents stood together. They had identical tolerating smiles. They were an imposing couple.

"Mama. Papa. This is Josh. Josh Flynn," Gwen explained simply.

Josh shook her father's hand.

"So you're the young man that lived next to us for a few years?" her father asked.

"Aye. I am," Josh said in his easy, friendly way. "It's nice to see you again."

"We thought we would stop by before going to the festivities," Gwen said lightly, trying to inch toward the door.

"No need to hurry, dear. We heard the inauguration isn't until noon," her mother said. "We'd like to visit with Mr. Flynn a while." She gave Josh a controlled smile and led the way to the study.

Gwen began to follow Josh and her parents, but her mother glanced over her shoulder and said, "Alone, if you please."

Gwen was shocked and tried to protest, but Josh gave her a wink of reassurance and trailed after them, having no idea he was a lamb being led to the slaughter. The door to the study shut soundly behind them.

Gwen perched on the edge of the sofa and waited for what seemed like an eternity. When she could stand it no longer, she went to the hallway, hoping to hear their conversation, but she could only make out muffled voices. She began to pace back and forth along the rug in the entryway. She felt it would be thread-bare by the time she heard enough commotion from the room to know they were about to emerge.

She hustled back to sit on the sofa just as the door opened. She looked at Josh questioningly, but he didn't appear to be in tatters. He was actually laughing at something her father said as they came into the parlor. Her mother seemed at peace. It was amazing.

"You two can run along and enjoy the day," her father commented. "But be back in time to get ready for the inaugural ball tonight."

"What?" Gwen was dumbfounded.

"We've decided to give the two of you our tickets to the ball," her mother informed her with a hint of a smile. "It's already been discussed. I'll find one of your father's old frock coats. It should fit Josh fine."

Gwen was stunned and speechless. It was an odd combination for her.

"Thank you, Mr. and Mrs. Sanders. We'll have a fine time," Josh said as he took Gwen by the elbow and ushered her out the front door.

"What? How?" Gwen sputtered when they were safely away. "What in the world did you talk to them about for so long?"

"Ah, that's for another time." He grinned. "Suffice it to say, you're not the only one with the powers of persuasion."

CHAPTER TWENTY-FIVE

Gwen could not believe the mass of humanity that was pressed together along Oklahoma Avenue in front of the Carnegie Library. With Josh's assistance, they were able to work their way close enough to see the wooden platform up high on the south steps. The choir from the orphanage was singing as they arrived. Josh put his hand protectively on her back. She felt secure knowing he was there to be a safeguard in case anyone became rowdy.

When Governor-elect Charles Haskell stepped out of the library, a great whoop sprang from the lips of the crowd. Everyone quieted down as he stood to the side while the entire presidential state proclamation was read aloud by another man.

After that, a man and woman came to the stage. The man represented Oklahoma Territory and the lady, Indian Territory. Mr. Oklahoma Territory gave a speech, somewhat humorous at times, wooing Miss Indian Territory so they could finally be joined in matrimony. The response came from another man on behalf of the maiden, extolling the virtues of Indian Territory and accepting the proposal. The couple was "married" to show that Oklahoma and Indian Territories were now joined as one state.

Gwen felt Josh slide his thumb along her shoulder blade as the couple on stage exchanged their mock vows. Gwen blushed, wondering if Josh still wanted to marry her. When she glanced up at him she could see deep affection for her in his eyes.

Mr. Haskell came forward and took his oath of office and gave his first address as governor of the new state of Oklahoma. As the ceremony progressed, more speeches were made and other officials were sworn in, including Kate Barnard, the commissioner of charities. It was quite a proud moment for Gwen, knowing that even though women couldn't vote yet, a young woman could be elected to an office.

After the formalities were over, a parade commenced with carriages for all the dignitaries. Mounted police, bands, cavalry troops, and militia rounded out the procession. Trailing at the end were a few automobiles. Gwen had to laugh when she saw Walter and Tina drive by. Tina was waving enthusiastically and looked pleased as punch.

Gwen pointed them out to Josh. "I don't think I broke his heart." She grinned up at the man by her side. "Tina probably already has him wrapped around her finger."

His mouth turned up, but he sounded serious as he asked, "It doesn't bother you, does it?"

She was going to give a light, funny answer, but she could see he really wanted complete honesty. "No. It doesn't. Not at all."

He appeared pensive for a moment before he grinned. "Good," he said.

The crowd began to follow the end of the parade toward Island Park, where barbecue, bread, and pickles were to be served for free.

"Do you want to go?" Gwen asked Josh.

"No. I've had enough elbow-rubbing for a while. How about some peace and quiet?"

"That sounds lovely. Let's go to the house. Mama is sure to have something for us to eat."

They walked in the opposite direction of the throng and were soon back at her parents' house. Her mother had kept some beef stew warm and even managed to save a few pieces of corn bread for them. They ate hungrily as her mother cleaned the kitchen. When they were finished, her mother informed them that she had made arrangements with Uncle Leo and Aunt Faye so Josh could spend the night there. She advised them to go visit so introductions could be made.

After a short respite, Gwen and Josh went to her uncle's house and visited with them for a long while. Aunt Faye plied them with pie and coffee in hopes of making Josh feel at ease. Josh seemed to enjoy her uncle's humor and her aunt's graciousness.

They stayed until it was dark. Gwen wanted to go back home to have plenty of time to get ready for the ball. When they arrived, her parents insisted on spending time with her and Josh.

Josh always appeared so at ease in whatever situation he was in. It was a quality she greatly admired in him. With only a tiny amount of trepidation, she tore herself away from his side and left him alone with her parents while she went up to begin her toilette.

Gwen went to the lavatory and washed up. She doused herself with powder since she wasn't fond of perfumes. She took the pins out of her long hair and brushed it out.

She went to her room and looked in her wardrobe. Deep in the recesses was a new gown she had been saving for a special occasion. She was so glad she hadn't worn it for Walter. She pulled it out and admired the soft, pale, shimmering rose-colored silk evening gown. It had a square neckline, elbow-length leg-of-mutton sleeves, and a corsage-style skirt with a medium sweep. The entire dress was trimmed in pristine white Irish lace. She laid it gently on the bed, disrobed, and began to slip into the new finery.

A soft knock came at the door.

"Do you need any assistance?" her mother's muffled voice asked.

Gwen let her mother in. She smiled. "Yes, I do. I'll need help with all these buttons at the back." She turned so her mother could begin on the long row.

"I haven't seen this dress before, have I?" her mother asked.

"No...I was keeping it for a momentous event," Gwen explained. "And..."

"And Walter wouldn't have appreciated the gown or the girl in it. Would he?" her mother asked sympathetically.

"No." Gwen twirled around and hugged her mother with tears in her eyes. "Thank you for understanding."

Her mother stepped back. "It took me time. And meeting Joshua today helped. I've never seen someone so smitten."

"Do you really think so?" Gwen couldn't help to ask.

Her mother smiled and nodded.

"I thought so too. But I wasn't sure." She was beginning to feel all aflutter just talking about it.

"He spoke rather eloquently about you earlier, Gwendolyn. He seems to be an exceptional man. Your father and I both approve of him," she said sincerely.

"Thank you, Mama." She was so happy to have had this private conversation. Knowing she had her parents' acceptance of Josh made the evening all the more special.

Her mother completed her task and said, "Now let's do your hair."

Gwen sat in her desk chair while her mother brushed her long brown locks.

"I've always wished I had hair as thick and luxurious as yours," her mother complimented her as she began to wind Gwen's hair up.

"Seriously?" Gwen hadn't known that. She really had never given her hair much thought.

"You'd be surprised how many young women use those false hairpieces to have the same look that you accomplish naturally." She placed pins in all the strategic places. "It's just about right. I'll return shortly."

Gwen slipped on her matching shoes while she waited. Her mother came back quickly and held up something sparkly.

"Your father gave this necklace to me when we became engaged." Her mother fastened the delicate gold chain with a diamond-encrusted heart pendant around Gwen's neck. "And this will be the perfect ornamentation." She placed a comb with rows of tiny diamonds in Gwen's hair in front of the bun on top. "Look." She took Gwen's hand and led her to the tall mirror. "You're just lovely, dear."

Gwen had never felt prettier. Squeezing her mother's hand, she savored the closeness she felt with her mother at that moment. She was so glad that she could see her mother as no longer an imagined foe but a friend.

"I believe Joshua is in full dress attire. I'll go down and tell him you are ready," her mother said as she left.

Gwen removed her white elbow-length gloves from the box on her chest of drawers and put them on. She smoothed out all the wrinkles and took a deep breath. She was utterly bursting with excitement. It wasn't the inaugural ball that she was enthusiastic about either. It was the fact that she was going to be spending an elegant evening with the most handsome, talented, hardworking man in the state. She couldn't wait another second.

~

Josh stood at the foot of the stairs with Gwen's parents. It was apparent he had won them over in spite of their earlier reservations. He was glad they had agreed to let him court their daughter, because that was what he intended to do.

He heard a rustling of skirts and peered up. His heart almost stopped when he saw how breathtaking Gwen was. He had never seen a woman more beautiful. Her skin was flawless and her dusky hair was silken. She was a glowing, picturesque combination of lights and darks in the flickering gaslights.

He placed his hand on his heart to ensure that it was indeed still beating as Gwen descended slowly. He could tell from her expression that she was as happy as he felt. As she neared, he held his hand out and guided her the rest of the way down.

"Here's your wrap, dear," Mrs. Sanders said, interrupting his thoughts. She placed a thick, fuzzy white shawl on Gwen's shoulders.

"Have a bully time," Mr. Sanders said when he opened the door for them.

"But don't stay out too late," Gwen's mother advised with a smile.

"Yes, ma'am." Josh reassured her quickly so he could have Gwen to himself again.

"Good-bye," Gwen said happily as they waved and strolled down the walkway and into the cool night air.

Gwen was silent for a moment before she glanced up at him and said almost shyly, "You are mighty handsome tonight, Mr. Flynn."

"Ah, 'tis only the cut of the clothes that have turned this simple man into a gentleman," he jested as he touched the brim of the top hat. He actually did feel a bit grander in the borrowed black frock coat, white vest, and white bow tie.

"Well, you're a gentleman regardless, but I do believe it's the cut of the man I like the most," she complimented him.

She spoke in a carefree manner, but he could hear the truthfulness behind her words. He stopped, turned to her, and grasped both of her hands in his.

"You are the most beautiful woman I have *ever* seen, Gwen. I wish I had the words to express it." He leaned closer until their lips were inches apart. He whispered, "If you'll let me, I would love to show you."

"We'll be the talk of the neighborhood," she mumbled.

"Does it matter?" he asked.

"No," she breathed.

He ran his fingers up her arm and neck and caressed her cheek before gently placing his lips on hers. She returned the kiss and he groaned. Gathering her into his arms, he felt himself melting into her. All of the years of waiting, hoping, and dreaming had finally passed and he felt the yearning for her—for this moment—in every fiber of his being.

He finally remembered that he was a gentleman and pulled himself away from her. "We've been apart far too long, Gwen."

Her gentle eyes held his and she sighed. "Yes. We have."

"Are you ready to make up for lost time?"

Gwen nodded.

He kissed her cheek quickly before placing her hand in the crook of his arm. "Then let's proceed to the ball, my love, and have the time of our lives."

CHAPTER TWENTY-SIX

Gwen thought she should pinch herself, but if the evening was a dream she didn't want to wake up. She stood in the ballroom of the convention hall and admired all the wreaths, garlands, palms, and starry chrysanthemums. The myriad of electric globes were almost hidden in vines and gave off a wonderful glow accentuating the exquisite colors of the ladies' gowns.

The crowd was immense. She had heard that at least two thousand attendees were milling around and dancing while the orchestra played from the balcony. Governor Haskell, his wife, and daughters had made their grand march earlier and were now standing in a receiving line.

Gwen had reluctantly let Josh leave her side to find some refreshments. While he was gone, she reminisced about their intimate moment. She had experienced being loved, cherished, and desired during that single kiss. It made her wobbly-kneed just thinking about it. The best thing of all was that she felt those exact same things for Josh. The overpowering sense of security, tenderness, and ardor that filled her made her feel so alive. She hated that she had missed those feelings for all those years, but she knew each step of her past had brought her to this moment in her life. She couldn't begrudge where she had been.

Gwen was beginning to wonder if Josh had gotten lost when Tina surfaced in front of her. She was dressed in a gold gown and she was grinning from ear to ear.

"Gwen! I thought I saw you earlier, but Walter didn't think so," Tina said enthusiastically. "Isn't this all stupendous?" She opened her arms wide and looked around.

"It certainly is," Gwen agreed.

"There's something I need to tell you, Gwen." Tina placed a gloved hand on Gwen's arm. Her eyes displayed a mixture of excitement and sympathy, as if she couldn't decide which emotion to show. "Walter and I are courting."

Gwen was silent, but her smile widened. She wasn't surprised by the announcement.

"Oh, I'm so glad you're not upset. Walter didn't think you would be, but he still didn't want me to say anything to you. But I didn't feel it was polite to not at least mention it so you wouldn't find out from someone else," she bubbled on and then changed her course as easily as a stormy brook. "I saw you with the *handsomest* man. Is he from Guthrie? Who is he?"

"He's a friend from Shawnee."

"Ohhh." She nodded knowingly. "There he comes! He *is* a handsome one, Gwen. Congratulations. As much as I'd like to be introduced, I'd better dash. Walter will think I've disappeared. Farewell," Tina said before she was engulfed by the crowd.

Josh finally made it to Gwen's side. He gave her a cup of punch. "Who was that wee bit of a girl?" he asked before taking a drink.

"No one important," she said rather smugly. It was a great satisfaction to finally not be jealous of Tina Randolph. She sipped her punch as a song ended and a waltz began.

"Are you ready for a turn around the floor?" Josh asked.

"I'll have to check my dance card." She pretended to look at the small card tied to her wrist. "Why, it appears all my dances are taken," she teased.

"Aye." He gave her a confident grin as he grabbed her hand. "They're taken by me."

He whirled her onto the dance floor and held her close as he expertly steered her through the other dancers. She absolutely relished his strong hand on her waist and clasping her fingers. He was surefooted and steady as he used gentle pressure to guide her to the rhythm of the music.

"My, you're quite the dancer, Mr. Flynn." She smiled up at him.

He chuckled. "Aye. And you should see me Irish jig. I was the talk of Kansas City."

She giggled and said, "I'm sure you were."

He deftly turned her to miss another couple, and they danced without conversation for a while. Every time she looked at Josh, she found him regarding her seriously. She had never seen any man express such affection in a single glance.

"What are you thinking?" she asked, almost feeling shy.

"Honestly?" His dark eyes held hers.

"Of course."

"I was thinking how proud I was to have such a lovely woman in my arms for all to see, but at the same instance I was wishing to be alone with you so no one *could* see us." There was a devilish twinkle in his eye.

"Oh." Gwen didn't know how to respond to that and felt herself turning pink instead. "I'm ready to leave if you are," she said sincerely.

"I was only teasing. This is something you've looked forward to for a long time."

"No." She pulled him to the side and leaned toward him. She whispered in his ear, "I've wanted *you* for a long time. I've been here long enough."

He inhaled sharply and gazed at her intently before breaking into a grin. "Let's get our things."

They found her wrap and Josh's borrowed hat and went out. The evening was turning chilly, and they walked close together. The electric streetlights illuminated their path as they ambled toward her parents' home. They could hear the raucous celebrating from the city's saloon patrons, who were having their last hurrah before the establishments had to close their doors for good at midnight. There was to be no more alcohol sold in the new state.

When they were home, Gwen grabbed Josh's hand and whispered, "I'm not ready for tonight to end. Let's go back here."

Moonlight and stars sparkled in the clear sky as she led him to the rear yard to a secluded bench in a corner. She sat and drew him down next to her. She shivered.

"Are you cold?" he asked.

She shook her head, but he put his arms around her shoulders anyway. He kissed her temple. "I never want to stop holding you," he said softly.

"And I never want you to let me go," she responded as she leaned into the warmth of his body.

"I thought I'd never hear you say that." He moved even closer and kissed her. His lips lingered on hers. He sighed as he tore himself away. "I didn't know what I'd do when you left. I wanted you, and I couldn't make you love me."

"I'm so sorry." She placed a gloved hand on his firm cheek. "Only time could make me see."

He nodded. His eyes all but burned into hers. "I love you, Gwen. I adore you, desire you, and *need* you. I can't live without you any longer. Will you marry me, Gwen? Will you spend the rest of your life with me as my wife? Will you let me love you now?"

"Yes. Yes. Yes." She kissed his rough cheek, the soft spot next to his eye, his lips. "Yes, to every question." She looked into his grateful eyes. "Yes, because...I've always loved *you*."

"It seems like I've waited an eternity to hear you say that." He put his fingers on her neck and his thumb stroked her jawline. "Do you want a long engagement?" he asked.

"No." She chuckled. "Definitely not."

"Let's get married before the year is out," he urged.

"Yes." Excitement filled every corner of her being. "December thirty-first, so we can spend the new year as husband and wife."

Josh jumped up, grabbed her, and twirled her around. "I'm the happiest man alive. I want to yell it to the rooftops. Gwen Sanders loves me!"

Gwen laughed. At last she could care less what others thought of her. She shouted, "And Josh Flynn loves me!"

They giggled like schoolchildren as a light came on in her parents' window. They grasped hands and ran around to the front steps.

He gave her a final embrace and kiss before he said softly, "When you get to your room, look out."

"I will." She smiled and gave him one last peck on the cheek before opening the door.

She glanced back at him and went in, running lightly up the stairs and into her room before her mother could stop her. She went through the semidarkness and held the curtain back from the window.

Josh was standing in the walkway. His hand was over his heart. When he saw her, he blew her a kiss and waved before turning and walking away with light steps.

She watched him until he disappeared into the darkness. Her heart was full of love and joy. Her childhood dreams had come true.

EPILOGUE

Gwen and Josh stood at the top of a long hill, bundled in coats as the strong winds buffeted them. They took in their surroundings. They observed the rock-walled parcels for farming, the sheep dotting the green landscape, and the small cottage in the valley that still belonged to some of Josh's kinfolk.

"I can't believe we're actually here," Gwen exclaimed as she peered up at her handsome husband.

"I know." He pulled her close. "I still feel a tad guilty about accepting Miss Duffy's offer for a honeymoon in Ireland."

Gwen nodded as she remembered the generosity of the woman she had barely met. She also recalled their beautiful wedding at St. Benedict's and how happy she had been to share the day with her family and friends. But nothing compared to where they were at this very moment.

She felt the flat gold wedding band press into her skin as she squeezed the hand that Josh had slipped around her waist. There was something comforting about wearing his grandmother Riley's ring that was engraved with Celtic trinity knots. She knew her marriage to Josh would be as happy as his grandparents' had been.

"'Tis good to be here," Josh murmured into her hair. "It's like we're home. Maybe we should just stay here."

She could tell by his light tone that he wasn't serious, but she agreed, "We just might have to. After all those days of seasickness, I'm in no hurry to go back."

He chuckled. "At least your affliction gave me time to read your wedding present. Your book was lovely."

"Thank you. It was only a story, though. What I'm excited about is writing our own epic together."

"You can bet it will have humor and fire and probably a bit of sadness..."

"But as long as we're side by side we'll conquer anything." Gwen faced him, placed her hands on his cheeks, and kissed him soundly.

Josh's eyes held hers. "Aye. That we will."

ABOUT THE AUTHOR

Sandra Wilkins is a passionate reader and writer of historical fiction, creating characters whose values reflect those she holds dear. She currently resides with her husband and two daughters in Oklahoma, where her family has lived for five generations. Wilkins homeschools her children and, when she isn't writing, she enjoys drawing, learning to play the guitar, and continuing to discover the world alongside her daughters. *Gwen's Honor* is her third novel, and she is busy working on her next series set in historical Chandler, Oklahoma.

Made in the USA
Lexington, KY
18 January 2013